"Go Get Dressed!"

Startled by his unexpectedly abrupt rejection, she got out of the pool and walked back to the pool house. Once inside, she didn't even switch on the light.

The door opened, and Jared was silhouetted in the moonlight. Clutching the towel around her, she stood immobile as he came across the room.

"Suzanne," he said huskily. "You don't really know what this all means."

Her cheeks coloured. "I'm only inexperienced, Jared, not ignorant."

DONNA VITEK

firmly believes that "I would probably have never learned to enjoy writing as much as I do" without the helpful influence of her husband. That love of writing has brought hours of enjoyment to her many fans, who eagerly await each new Silhouette by this talented author.

Dear Reader,

Silhouette Romances is an exciting new publishing series, dedicated to bringing you the very best in contemporary romantic fiction from the very finest writers. Our stories and our heroines will give you all you want from romantic fiction.

Also, *you* play an important part in our future plans for Silhouette Romances. We welcome any suggestions or comments on our books, which should be sent to the address below.

So enjoy this book and all the wonderful romances from Silhouette. They're for *you*!

Jane Nicholls
Silhouette Books
PO Box 177
Dunton Green
Sevenoaks
Kent
TN13 2YE

DONNA VITEK

Sweet Surrender

Silhouette *Romance*

Published by Silhouette Books

Copyright © 1982 by Donna Vitek

Map by Tony Ferrara

First printing 1983

British Library C.I.P.

Vitek, Donna
    Sweet surrender.—(Silhouette romance)
    I. Title
    813'.54[F]   PS3543.I/

    ISBN 0 340 33264 6

Printed and bound in Great Britain for
Hodder and Stoughton Paperbacks, a
division of Hodder and Stoughton Ltd.,
Mill Road, Dunton Green, Sevenoaks,
Kent (Editorial Office: 47 Bedford
Square, London, WC1 3DP) by
Richard Clay (The Chaucer Press) Ltd.,
Bungay, Suffolk

For Madge James Johnson

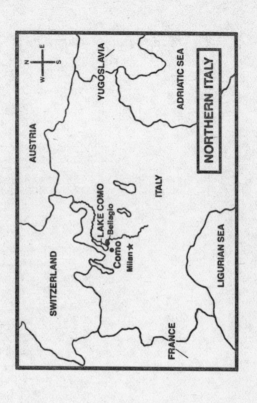

Chapter One

Suzanne Collins strummed her fingers restlessly on the arms of her chair. After another half minute of watching her friend Lynn ogle the handsome young interns who were continually passing up and down the hall, Suzanne quietly stood and started to fold a nightgown, only to have the other girl snatch it out of her hands.

"Sit back down right now," Lynn commanded as she folded the gown haphazardly. "I don't need you to help me pack these things. You're supposed to take it easy. You've been sick."

"But I'm fine now," Suzanne insisted, though she did sit down again and a smile danced in her emerald green eyes. "Besides, you seem far more interested in flirting with the doctors than in packing my suitcase so I just thought I'd give you some help. I *am* rather anxious to see the last of this place."

"No, you're just a compulsive doer," Lynn argued good-naturedly, tossing a pair of fabric slippers into the suitcase. "I'd be quite content to lounge in this hospital bed for a week or so and flirt with the interns but you can't wait to get back to the apartment, where I'm sure you'll decide there are a million things you have to do. The trouble is you try to do more than one thing at a time. That's what landed you in the hospital in the first place, remember? It wasn't enough that you were studying for exams. You had to get some fresh air and exercise at the same time by hiking halfway up the mountain. Well, you got some fresh air all right *and* pneumonia."

"Oh, stop fussing like a mother hen," Suzanne retorted. "I like to study outside. How was I to know I was going to be caught in a sudden deluge of rain? Besides, it's nearly June; the weather was nice and warm. If I hadn't had a cold anyway. . . ." She shrugged. "Well, it was only a slight case of pneumonia."

"Slight! There's no such thing as a slight case of *double* pneumonia." Shaking her head, Lynn rolled her eyes heavenward. "In case you don't remember, you were a pretty sick girl when I finally managed to drag you in to the emergency room. Why else do you think the doctor kept you here for a week?"

"Please, no more sermonizing. Will you just pack my things so we can go?" Suzanne persisted, gazing longingly out the window. "It seems like a million years since I was out in the sunshine. I can hardly wait to go for a long walk."

"Hmmph! You'll think the walk up the two flights of stairs to our apartment is plenty long enough," Lynn muttered. "You don't realize how weak a bout with pneumonia can make you. But *I* had it three years ago and I know I tended to get tired very easily for a month or two afterward. Didn't the doctor tell you that you'd have to take it easy?"

"He didn't tell me I'd have to act like an invalid and I don't want you trying to treat me like one." Squaring her shoulders and jaw determinedly, Suzanne smoothed back a strand of silken auburn hair that had escaped the neat chignon on her nape. "So hurry up with the packing, please. I can't wait to get home and wash this hair of mine."

"Wash you hair!" Lynn exclaimed, then shook her head emphatically. "Oh, no, you can't possibly wash your hair yet; you'll make yourself sick again."

"Not if I blow dry it. And I am going to wash it," Suzanne argued calmly, giving her friend an indulgent smile. "My, you certainly have gotten bossy since your birthday. You seem to be forgetting I'll be twenty-one next month, too, so you might as well stop trying to treat me like a child. You'll have to find somebody else to adopt." She grinned teasingly. "I'm beginning to think you have some very strong subconscious maternal longings that are beginning to surface. Maybe you should consider getting married and having a baby."

"Very funny," Lynn rejoined, though she was grinning too. "But if I decide I need to have myself psychoanalyzed, I think I'll see a professional, thank you. Besides, I'm not trying to mother you. I just want you to get well fast so you can start doing your share of the chores at the apartment again."

Wrinkling her nose in response, Suzanne sat back in her chair and watched as her friend finally put the last gown in the suitcase, snapped shut the clasps, then put it on the floor at the foot of the bed. "Well, we're ready to go. As soon as the doctor comes to check—" Lynn's words halted abruptly with the sudden outbreak of a commotion up the hall. Several people were obviously all trying to talk at one time and their voices were becoming increasingly louder and more strident. Throwing Suzanne a puzzled look, Lynn went to the open door to peer up the corridor, then jumped back suddenly and spun around to face her friend. Her mouth was nearly hanging open with surprise but she snapped it shut again and gestured excitedly. "Oh my gosh, you'll never guess who's walking down the hall this very minute! The Empress!"

Suzanne tensed and her cheeks paled slightly.

"Delia?" she asked softly, a hard knot developing in the pit of her stomach. "But it can't be Delia! She's in Italy with my father. Are you sure it isn't just somebody who resembles her? Look again."

"I don't have to look again," Lynn whispered dramatically as she darted across the room, long chestnut hair streaming out behind her. "It's the Empress, all right. Nobody in the world walks down a hall like she does, as if she's making a grand entrance at her own coronation."

"Oh heavens, I think I might have a relapse," Suzanne groaned. "What's she doing here? She's certainly never made a habit of seeking me out. I can't imagine what she possibly wants."

"You're about to find out," Lynn drawled. Then she added out of the corner of her mouth, "Are we supposed to grovel at her feet or will a curtsy suffice?"

"A curtsy will be sufficient. I think," Suzanne murmured; then she straightened in her chair as her stepmother swept into the room.

Clad in a white silk suit, Delia Collins was blatantly overdressed for a visit to a hospital, especially one in a small Vermont university town, but she was not a woman who let such minor details bother her. Glancing around the room with its spartan, strictly utilitarian furnishings, she patted the smooth cap of her jet black hair and turned up her nose in disgust. "Hospitals and clinics do have the most obnoxious smell and those bossy nurses didn't even want to let me in because it isn't visiting hour," she declared heatedly, then turned her cold brown eyes on the two girls by the window. After acknowledging Lynn with a reluctant nod, she turned her full attention toward her stepdaughter and sniffed disparagingly. "Well, I've never seen you look worse, dear. And I really was surprised to hear you were sick; you've always been such a robust little thing.

10

Why did you pick late spring as the time to catch pneumonia, of all things?"

"Oh, I just thought it might be a fun thing to do," Suzanne replied, a hint of sarcasm in her voice. Ignoring Lynn, who was smiling behind her hand, she steadily met her stepmother's disdainful glare. "To what do I owe the pleasure of this visit, Delia? I thought you were in Italy with Dad."

Nodding perfunctorily, Delia settled herself on the spare chair by the bed, crossing her long tanned legs, then lifting one up slightly so she could more easily admire the snakeskin pump on her foot. "I *was* in Italy with Jack, of course, and I'm really enjoying living there. I've met some delightful people and there seems to be a party somewhere every night," she chattered, then suddenly frowned, apparently realizing she had strayed from the original topic. "Well, anyway, I'm only here now because when we tried to call you at your apartment, no one ever answered. So, finally I called your dean of women and she told me you were in the hospital. Of course, Jack got all in a dither and insisted I come and make sure you were all right."

"Well, as you can see, I'm better now," Suzanne said. "But if Dad was so worried, why didn't he come see me himself? And why were you trying to reach me anyway?"

For a few seconds, Delia was too intent on examining a chip in the crimson polish on one long fingernail to answer, but at last she glanced up and announced with characteristic bluntness, "Jack thought you should be told that he suffered a minor heart seizure last Thursday. Just a teeny one really, not very serious."

"Not very serious!" Suzanne's voice quavered as her eyes widened in dismay. "Any sort of heart problem is serious, Delia. Is he okay? What does his doctor say?"

"What does any doctor ever say?" Delia delicately

flicked her wrist, making a nonchalant gesture with her hand. "They never talk so anybody can understand them and, heavens, this one was Italian too! His English was terrible—I hardly understood a word he was saying. If Jared hadn't been there to handle everything for me, I probably wouldn't have known Jack could come home day before yesterday."

"Oh, thank heaven he's well enough to be home," Suzanne murmured, able now to take a deep breath and release it in a shuddering sigh of relief. "But how's he feeling?"

"Worried about you, of course," Delia snapped, as if she thought Suzanne had caught pneumonia deliberately to upset him. "But now that I see you're perfectly fine I'll catch a plane back to Rome tomorrow, tell him the good news, and he'll stop fretting about you. He needs to regain his strength so our lives can begin to get back to normal."

"You won't have to tell him I'm fine," Suzanne said, rising swiftly to her feet. "He'll be able to see for himself that I'm better because I'm going back to Italy with you."

Delia scowled, her crimson-glossed lips thinning. "But I don't think Jack expects you to leave your sickbed just to come see him. No, indeed. In fact, I'm sure he doesn't want you to. My goodness, dear," she added, trying to sound friendlier but not succeeding. "You can't travel right now. After all, you've just had pneumonia. Your father would never forgive himself if you became sick again because you felt you should visit him."

"I don't just feel like I should; I *want* to see him and I'm going to," Suzanne answered firmly with an uptilting of her small chin. Despite her slight build and petite stature, she possessed an inner strength and independence that revealed themselves in her clear green eyes.

It was a strength she had developed of necessity when her mother died. Even two years later, when she was fifteen and her father married Delia after an impetuous, whirlwind courtship, Suzanne never let her stepmother intimidate her and she wasn't about to let her start now. "What time does the flight for Rome leave tomorrow?" she asked, steadily meeting Delia's irritated scowl until at last the older woman looked away and jerked open the snap closure of her snakeskin clutch purse. After finding a jeweled compact and a tube of crimson lip gloss, she began painstakingly to redo her mouth.

"The flight leaves at ten in the morning. An outrageous hour," she muttered. "But I still think you should stay here. Your father isn't all that ill. He can do without seeing you."

"But I can't do without seeing him," Suzanne countered flatly. Glancing at Lynn, she received an understanding smile which she gratefully returned. "And what would you do in my place, Lynn?" she asked rather perversely, knowing what the answer would be. "Would you stay here?"

"I'd do exactly what you're going to do; I'd go see my father no matter what," the other girl said. "But I'm not so sure what your doctor will have to say about your going. We'll just have to wait and see."

As it turned out, the wait ended within a minute or so when Dr. Bradwell, a handsome middle-aged man, a bit stern yet kindly, strode into Suzanne's room. After politely telling Delia and Lynn they must step into the hall for a moment, he listened through his stethoscope to Suzanne's breathing. "Clear of congestion," he pronounced. As she rebuttoned her blouse, he gazed musingly out the window. "In my opinion, the discovery of antibiotics is the greatest milestone thus far in the history of medicine. If you'd lived forty years ago, you wouldn't have lasted long with the severe case of pneumonia you had. Don't forget that, Suzanne; don't ever yearn to have lived in the past, when everything was supposedly simpler and therefore better."

She smiled at him. "No, I don't imagine the good old days were nearly as good as some people want to believe they were. I'm quite content to be living right now, today."

"I always suspected you were a sensible girl," he commented as he went to the door and informed Lynn and Delia that they could return to the room. Then, hands in his trouser pockets, he rocked back and forth on his feet, surveying his patient intently. "All right, since you're dressed already and so eager to escape, I'm releasing you. But . . ." His expression grew sterner. "No strenuous activity for at least three weeks. And I mean that! Don't decide to start training for a marathon. In a week to ten days, you can resume all your *regular* activities but don't try to do more physically than you're accustomed to doing. All right? And for the next week, at least, don't do anything really tiring at all."

"Then I don't think she should try to fly to Europe tomorrow, do you, doctor?" Delia spoke up, her tone huskier and her expression discernibly more pleasant as she gazed up at the man. It was as if she had flipped a switch and become a brand-new Delia, a Delia who knew how to charm and manipulate men. Or at least she knew how to give it a good try. As she smiled too sweetly up at Dr. Bradwell, she actually reached out and stroked Suzanne's hair. "She's been such a sick little girl, hasn't she? I don't think she should try to make such a long trip, do you?"

"My father's ill," Suzanne explained hastily. "He's in Italy now and of course I want to see him. I have to go, Dr. Bradwell."

"I see." Nodding, the doctor tapped his chin thoughtfully. "Well, I understand why you have to go, but try to sleep on the plane. Try not to—"

"You can't mean you're giving her permission?" Delia interrupted rather shrilly, impatience emphasizing the fine lines around her mouth and between her brows. "You've just said she shouldn't do anything tiring for a week! How can you think of letting her fly to Europe?"

Dr. Bradwell's glasses had slipped down on his nose and now he stared at Delia over the top of the frames, as he asked tersely, "Are you Suzanne's mother?"

Delia was horrified at the question. For a moment, her cheeks hollowed with her swiftly indrawn breath and her skin flushed an angry red, but at last she managed to control herself enough to giggle rather stupidly. Pursing her lips in an exaggerated pout, she waggled a finger at the doctor. "You naughty thing, you're teasing me. You know I couldn't possibly be Suzanne's mother. After all, she's nearly twenty-one and I'm only thirty-two. You know I don't look old enough to be her mother. Now, do I?"

When Dr. Bradwell studiously avoided the question, his silence became an answer in itself, one that didn't put Delia in a very good humor. She glared at Suzanne, then followed the doctor as he started out the door to go sign the release form at the nurse's station.

"Wait," Lynn called before either of them could reach the door. "Mrs. Collins, you must have rented a car to drive here, would you mind dropping Suzanne and me off at our apartment? I don't think she should have to sit outside waiting for a bus."

Delia hesitated, obviously not overjoyed at the idea of giving them a lift. "Well," she muttered finally, "I was planning to go find a motel room for tonight."

"Fine, you can drop us off on your way to look for

one." Lynn turned amused blue eyes toward the doctor. "You don't want Suzanne sitting on a bench, waiting for a bus, do you?"

"Most certainly not," he declared emphatically, glancing expectantly at Delia.

Having previously put on the loving stepmother act, she was now trapped. Never one to show her true character to any man, she at last had to agree to drive the girls to their apartment. But the venomous look she bestowed on both of them proved beyond a doubt that she strongly resented the inconvenience.

By eight o'clock that evening, Suzanne found she was still feeling well. A bit tired but not excessively weary. She could hardly believe that only four days ago she had felt so badly. As she sat on the comfortable brown tweed sofa in the small living room of the apartment and gazed at her seashell collection on the bookcase across from her, she was wondering if Dr. Bradwell hadn't perhaps exaggerated the dangers of overexerting herself. She felt fine, almost restless in fact, but when she had proposed to help Lynn wash the dinner dishes, the other girl had flatly refused to allow it. Lynn was a great friend and Suzanne felt as close to her as if she were the sister she had always longed for when she was a child. Sitting on the sofa, remembering the good times they had had together, Suzanne smiled as Lynn pushed open the swinging kitchen door and stepped into the living room.

Lynn grinned back mischievously, then proceeded to strut across the living room, her hips swaying provocatively as her pixie face took on a very haughty expression. "Sleep on the sofa?" she mimicked Delia very convincingly. "Oh, I think not. You girls are accustomed to this . . . apartment but I think I would be much more comfortable in a motel room. I do presume there are decent motels to be found, even in this small town?"

Suzanne had to laugh. "I really think you should consider becoming a professional impressionist, Lynn. You sound just like Delia, and even look a little like her by putting on that snooty expression. I get the vague idea you don't like her very much."

"What's to like?" Lynn countered bluntly, flopping down in a well-worn overstuffed easy chair. Swinging her legs over one armrest, she lounged back. "In case you hadn't noticed, your stepmother is a fake through and through. I wonder how much it costs her a month to keep her hair so raven black."

Suzanne grimaced. "I hate to tell you this but I think that's her natural hair color, though she did begin to get a few gray strands a couple of years ago. She probably touches it up now to keep it as dark as it used to be."

"Too bad she doesn't do some touching up on her personality." Sniffing, Lynn swung one foot as if she were rather agitated. "She's horrendous. Didn't you want to smack her when she stroked your hair, trying to act like she's such a concerned stepmother? If she was trying to impress Dr. Bradwell, I'm not sure she succeeded."

"I doubt it. He seems too perceptive a man to be taken in by insincerity."

Lynn suddenly laughed gleefully. "Well, he certainly didn't win any love from her when he asked if she were your mother. For a minute, I thought she was going to explode. And I don't think he was convinced when she told him she was only thirty-two. Just how old is she anyway?"

"I don't really know," Suzanne said, spreading her hands in an expressive gesture. "Age isn't something she seems to want to discuss. I suppose Dad knows how old she is but I've never asked him."

"How could you?" Lynn retorted angrily. "She proved today that she doesn't want you to see him, if she can help it. And she's always tried to keep the two of you apart, hasn't she?"

"When she married Dad, she didn't seem exactly thrilled to be my stepmother but, in all fairness, I can't blame her for the lack of closeness between my father and me. After Mother died, he just sort of withdrew. I thought we needed each other more than ever, but he tried to lose himself in his work. Then when Jared became his partner about six years ago, Dad began traveling so much that I saw even less of him. And when he married Delia . . . well . . ." Suzanne smiled pensively. "Actually, I feel more at home with your family than I ever do with Dad and her."

"Well, you know that Mom loves to have you visit," Lynn offered sincerely, then wrinkled her brow quizzically. "So this Jared Delia kept talking about today is your father's partner? She couldn't seem to shut up about him. Is he that terrific?"

Suzanne shrugged. "I've only seen him a couple of times, the last time was about three years ago. He seemed nice."

"I wonder what his wife thinks about his spending so much time helping dear Delia get through your father's illness," Lynn said rather sharply. "If I were a wife, I sure wouldn't want my husband spending many hours with that woman."

Laughing again, Suzanne shook her head. "Jared Caine isn't married. At least, he wasn't three years ago."

"Oh, really?" Lynn questioned, sitting up straighter. "He's young, didn't you say? How young?"

"Somewhere in his early thirties, I guess. Why?"

"And how does he look?"

"Well, I was very impressed with him three years ago but I was only eighteen," Suzanne replied wryly. "He's tall, dark, maybe not classically handsome but certainly attractive." Her eyebrows lifted inquiringly. "Why all these questions?"

"Delia sounded very interested in him," Lynn responded, then grimaced apologetically. "You don't think. . . ."

"No!" Suzanne shook her head emphatically, though a fleeting anguish crossed over her delicate features. "No, she couldn't be involved with Jared. I know Delia has her faults and plenty of them but she . . . surely she wouldn't actually have an affair."

"You're probably right," Lynn hastened to agree though she didn't sound particularly convinced. Nor did she credit Delia with very noble motives for remaining faithful to Jack Collins. "After all, he's got enough money to keep the Empress relatively content. As long as she can go out on her shopping sprees, I don't imagine she'll give him a lot of trouble."

"You really have to stop calling her the Empress around me," Suzanne chided halfheartedly, though a hint of a smile tugged at her softly shaped lips. "It's gotten to the point where I think of her as the Empress myself. If I'm not careful I'll slip up and call her that while I'm in Italy."

"Don't forget to curtsy when you do. Empresses tend to get miffed when they aren't shown the proper respect," Lynn said tartly. Her expression immediately sobered. "You know, it's going to be very quiet around here without you. How long do you think you'll stay in Italy?"

"That really depends on Dad," Suzanne murmured, idly pleating the hem of her white cotton robe between her fingers. "If he seems to want me around, I'll stay as long as he needs me. Since Dr. Bradwell told me I should skip the summer semester anyway and regain my strength, I won't need to rush back here, though I did plan to design and make batik curtains for the apartment."

"Instead you'll be enjoying romantic Italy while I'll be stuck here improving my mind with literature courses," Lynn complained enviously. "I'll only have two weeks off all summer and I'll be spending those with my family at Niagara Falls, of all places. Doesn't it sound thrilling?"

Suzanne's eyes brightened. "I have a terrific idea. Why don't you persuade your parents to let you come to Italy to visit me, if I'm still there then? I'll certainly be in need of some company if I stay that long. Do you think they'd let you go?"

Lynn grimaced. "The airfare would be pretty expensive."

"You could remind them how educational a trip to Italy would be," Suzanne reminded her with a grin. "And besides, you'd be staying with us so you wouldn't have to pay for a hotel room or for food. All in all, it would be a relatively inexpensive European trip."

"Umm, that's true," Lynn agreed thoughtfully, then laughed and lifted her shoulders in a slight shrug. "Oh, what the heck, it certainly wouldn't hurt to ask them if they'd finance the trip. If they agreed, the two of us could really have a nice time sight-seeing together, couldn't we?"

"It might be the only bright moment of the summer for me," Suzanne remarked candidly. "Dad and I just aren't close anymore. I never really know what to say to him. And, of course, Delia and I don't communicate at all. Frankly, Lynn, I really dread going. I want to be with Dad because he's ill but. . . ." She paused a moment, shaking her head, as if reassembling her thoughts. "You know, I'd prefer to go with you and your family to Niagara Falls. I'm sure I'd have a better time there with all of you than I'll have in Italy, knowing Delia doesn't want me there for a minute."

"Oh, don't let the Empress bother you." Lynn dispensed with Suzanne's stepmother with a derogatory wave of one hand. "She's just a shrew. Forget about her while you're there. Okay?"

"I'll try," Suzanne answered, examining her fingernails pensively as she added, "You know, I still don't understand why Dad ever married Delia. She's nothing like my mother was and he loved Mother so much. Wonder why he didn't marry someone more like her, someone quiet and unselfish and loving? Why a cold fish like Delia? She's Mother's opposite in nearly every way imaginable."

"Maybe that's exactly why he married her—because she is so different," Lynn suggested surprisingly. "My Uncle Joel did the same thing when Aunt Jean died. He married a silly little twit, but my mother said she thought he did it deliberately. He was lonely, but since he knew he wouldn't find anyone who could take Aunt Jean's place, he married someone he knew was very different. He didn't expect much from her besides companionship, so he wasn't disappointed when he didn't get any more than that."

"I never thought of it that way," Suzanne said softly, nibbling her lower lip. "How sad for Dad to know he'll never be as happy again as he was with Mother. But . . . I guess he was lucky to have had such a wonderful relationship even once in his life. Some people never do. Those are the ones to pity, I guess." With a half smile, she stared at the floor silently for a long moment, then roused herself from her reverie to glance at the clock. She gave Lynn an apologetic smile. "I know it's only nine o'clock but I think I'll go to bed now. I have to get up early in the morning to finish packing and tomorrow's going to be a horrendously long day—I'll have to spend all of it with Delia."

"Heaven help you," Lynn retorted only half teasing. She stretched her arms above her head as Suzanne stood. "I may go to bed soon myself. The few hours I spent with the Empress today have tired me out so I can imagine how you must be feeling."

"I just need a good night's sleep; I'm sure I'll be feeling fine in the morning," Suzanne murmured, hiding a small yawn behind one hand as she walked to the open door of her bedroom. "Good night, Lynn."

Also yawning now, Lynn nodded but before Suzanne could walk into her room, she called after her. "Don't let the Empress spoil your visit with your father. And don't let her spoil your enjoyment of Italy. Remember what a romantic country it's supposed to be. You might even fall madly in love while you're there."

"Well, I certainly don't count on that happening," Suzanne responded with a wry grin. "If Delia has her way, I probably won't even meet any men while I'm there. She's never been particularly eager to include me in her social activities."

"She wouldn't. She's the kind of rotten stepmother that gives them all a bad name," Lynn assessed bitingly, then gave Suzanne an encouraging smile. "Just try not to let her make you miserable."

"I've never let her make me miserable yet. I don't plan to start now," Suzanne answered with a slight uptilting of her small chin. "I learned when I was fifteen to ignore her as much as possible. So don't worry about me; I'll be fine in Italy."

"And you'll try to enjoy yourself?" Lynn persisted. "It's not every summer you get to go to Europe. You never know—you *might* meet a terrific man and fall in love. Wouldn't that be exciting?"

"I never knew until this moment what a hopeless romantic you are," Suzanne countered, smiling indulgently. "But I'm going to Italy to see Dad. That's all. If you want to daydream though, be my guest. But I'm afraid you'll have to do it alone tonight. I'm really sleepy."

"If you're going to be such a stick-in-the-mud, I'm not sure I want to come join you in Italy," Lynn retorted but she returned Suzanne's smile as she stepped into her bedroom and closed the door behind her.

The flight to Rome was long and tedious. While Suzanne tried to occupy most of the time by reading, Delia slept, even through the serving of lunch. Unfortunately, she awakened in time for dinner in one of her most unpleasant moods. After meticulously tidying her hair and reapplying lip gloss, she launched into an endless string of complaints. It was too cold in the plane; the flight was bumpy and the dinner served in the first class section was, according to her, practically inedible though Suzanne thought the steak and lobster entree delicious.

"Everything on my tray was cold," Delia pronounced critically to the flight attendant who came to take her tray away. "Considering the cost of my plane ticket, I certainly did expect to be served a decent meal, especially here in first class."

"I'm sorry you didn't enjoy dinner," the unruffled young woman replied. Turning her attention to Suzanne, she raised her eyebrows questioningly. "And was your food cold, too, Miss Collins?"

"Oh, no, it was fine," Suzanne answered, ignoring Delia's withering stare. "I thought everything was delicious, in fact."

"Well, my food was cold," Delia reiterated with a disgusted sniff. "And you can be sure I'll tell all my friends what a disaster this meal was so they'll know to avoid flying this airline in the future."

The flight attendant grimaced apologetically. "I'm sorry you're dissatisfied with the service. If only you'd mentioned that your food was cold, we would have been glad to bring you another tray."

"It's a little late to tell me that now, don't you think?" Delia retorted rather sarcastically. "But I do think you owe me a drink for my inconvenience. You can bring me a champagne cocktail."

"Yes, ma'am, right away," the stewardess said pleasantly, obviously undaunted by Delia's rather rude behavior. Unfortunately, she also gave Suzanne a friendly smile and innocently added, "How about you, Miss Collins? Would you like me to bring you something when I return with your mother's champagne cocktail?"

Delia was incensed. Jerking up her head, she drawled cattily, "Perhaps you should have your eyesight checked, dear. Take a closer look and surely you'll see I couldn't possibly be the mother of a twenty-one-year-old girl."

Delia's voice had risen slightly and it carried to the occupants in the surrounding seats. As they observed the scene curiously, the flight attendant spread her hands in an uncertain gesture. Realizing the mistake she had made, she said sincerely, "I'm truly sorry, Mrs. Collins. I didn't mean to upset you. I just assumed since your names are the same. . . . And, after all, Miss Collins really doesn't look like she could be twenty-one." She grimaced, then turned a helpless gaze on Suzanne. "I mean. . . . Oh, dear, I hope *you* didn't mind my saying *that*."

"No problem," Suzanne assured her, smiling sympathetically. "And no thank you, don't bring anything for me."

"Are you going to bring my drink or not?" Delia said huffily, glaring up at the stewardess. I certainly could use one, especially now."

After murmuring another apology, the flight attendant eagerly escaped. As she hurried down the narrow aisle toward the galley, Delia muttered something beneath her breath and Suzanne hastily opened her book again, hoping to disassociate herself from her stepmother by ignoring her completely if she could.

Unfortunately, she couldn't. Delia had altogether different intentions. Swinging around in her seat, she began a verbal assault. "You really have to do something about the way you look, Suzanne," she declared, surveying her disdainfully. "Why do you want to go around looking fourteen years old? Good heavens, you're almost twenty-one. Don't you think you ought to look a little more sophisticated?"

With a resigned sigh, Suzanne looked up reluctantly from her book. "I'm sure I look older than fourteen, Delia," she answered calmly. "And if my appearance irritates you, then I'm sorry, but I really don't know how I can change it."

"Well for one thing, you could do something with that hair of yours."

"My hair?" Automatically, Suzanne touched the soft sweep of auburn hair that was held back from her face by gold barrettes. "What's wrong with my hair?"

"Everything. Have it cut and styled so that your face doesn't look so little girlish. Good heavens, you're absolutely lacking in sophistication. But a chic hairstyle would make you look a little more your age. I've found a perfectly divine hair stylist in Milan. I'll take you to him, maybe tomorrow. I'm sure he'll be able to do something to improve you."

"Thanks, but no thanks," Suzanne said flatly. "I'm satisfied with my hair the way it is. I have no desire to have it cut."

"Well, you can't expect to look your age if you let that hair swing around your shoulders like you're Alice in Wonderland," Delia persisted. "And sweeping it back from your face that way makes your eyes look too . . . too childish and it certainly doesn't help to conceal that sprinkling of freckles across your nose and cheekbones. You could get rid of those permanently, though, by having a chemical peel."

"A chemical peel?" Suzanne wondered softly, her green eyes widening in disbelief. "You must be kidding! I'm not fond of my freckles but I certainly don't hate them so much I'd risk a chemical peel. Good grief, I've read that people have been permanently scarred by that procedure."

Delia tossed one hand in a dismissive gesture. "Scare stories. I'm sure chemical peels very rarely go wrong."

"Fine. Then you go have one done on your face—I'm not about to," Suzanne retorted, her patience wearing thin. "And as for the rest of my appearance, you'll just have to learn to live with it. I am what I am and since I'm relatively satisfied with the way I look, I don't plan to make any drastic changes, especially not to suit you."

A deep scowl furrowed Delia's forehead as her brown eyes grew harder still. "You know what I think? I think you love it when people assume you're my daughter," she whispered furiously. "So you try to look as young as possible just to irritate me."

"Since I rarely see you, that would be rather foolish on my part, don't you think?" Suzanne responded as coolly as possible. "Contrary to what you may believe, my life doesn't revolve around you. I certainly don't deliberately look young just to cause you aggravation. I keep my hair long because it's easy to care for that way, and as for the freckles, I've had them for as long as I can remember. They didn't just pop out on my face to spite you when you married my father."

"And I didn't say they did. I—"

"This whole conversation is ridiculous," Suzanne interrupted tautly, turning away and reopening the book in her lap. "Now, if you'll excuse me, I'd like to get on with my reading. I'm in the middle of a very exciting chapter."

"I intend to tell your father exactly how rude you've been to me," Delia announced threateningly. "And he won't be pleased, you can count on that." With a toss of her head that didn't disturb one strand of her hair, she got up and marched down the aisle toward the first-class lounge.

Luckily for Suzanne, Delia didn't return to her seat until the plane was about to land at the airport in Rome. Even then, the two of them said nothing further to each other. The tense silence was a relief to Suzanne, yet a source of concern too. She had hoped her relationship with her stepmother wouldn't become this strained so early in her visit to Italy. Yet it had, and now there was little she could do except try to avoid Delia as much as possible.

Forty minutes later, when they had left the plane and gone through customs, Delia made it clear she had no desire to remain in Suzanne's company either. Thrusting the handle of her red leather cosmetic case into Suzanne's hand, she made a beeline for the exit gate and the tall, broad-shouldered man in a tan vested suit who stood on the other side.

Recognizing Jared Caine, Suzanne followed in her wake. Carrying both her own tote bag and purse and Delia's ridiculously heavy cosmetic case, she walked slowly, suddenly feeling rather weary. And it was a weariness that combined with bewilderment when she passed through the gate and Jared Caine's black eyes turned in her direction to sweep relentlessly over the slender length of her body. Heat tingled in her cheeks as she imagined she detected something akin to dislike or disapproval tighten the chiseled features of his sunbrowned face. Certain that tiredness was making her overly imaginative, she gave him a rather shy smile which faded from her lips when it wasn't returned. Hardly encouraged by his lack of response, Suzanne stopped a few feet from where he stood with Delia and said quietly, "It's nice to see you again, Mr. Caine."

"I'm glad you decided to come visit your father, Miss Collins," was his answer but the tone of his deep voice was no more friendly than the expression on his tanned face.

Chapter Two

"How is my father?" Suzanne asked, shifting the heavy cosmetic case from one hand to the other. "Have you seen him today, Mr. Caine?"

"I have not seen him. But I did talk to him earlier this evening and he said he was feeling perfectly fine," Jared informed her, a hint of a smile playing over his firmly shaped mouth. "Actually he was complaining bitterly because the doctor won't allow him out of bed yet."

"Isn't that just like Jack?" Delia purred, sidling closer to Jared to grip his forearm with clinging, possessive hands. The bright lights in the airport terminal shimmered in her gleaming hair as she smiled up at him, then glanced sideways at her stepdaughter. "I suppose Jack's all excited about Suzanne's visit. I really didn't think she was going to come back with me. I was quite surprised when she decided she would. It's so sweet of you to come here to meet me . . . us. I did so dread arriving in Rome late at night, but since you're here. . . ."

"I had business in Rome anyway," Jared commented. "I told Jack I'd be glad to meet your plane and reserve rooms for both of you at the hotel where I'm staying. All right with you?"

"Anything you say, Jared," Delia murmured, her

voice taking on a husky resonance. Delia's expertly made-up eyes gazed adoringly at him, her crimson-tipped fingers stroking his arm. "You're so sweet to me. I don't know what I'd do without you."

Watching her stepmother, Suzanne was struck forcibly by the unbidden memory of Lynn's suggestion that perhaps Delia and Jared were having an affair. Certainly, Delia seemed to have more than a friendly interest in her husband's business partner! Suzanne found herself suddenly wondering why he had happened to be in Rome the very night Delia was flying in from New York. Perhaps tonight was supposed to be a lover's rendezvous—that would explain Jared's antagonistic attitude toward Suzanne. He *had* sounded as if he hadn't really expected her to come to Italy; maybe he resented the intrusion. But no, Suzanne thought desperately, he and Delia just couldn't be having an affair. Though she personally knew little about Jared Caine, she did remember hearing her father say many times that Jared was the most honest and trustworthy business partner he had ever had.

Suzanne bent her head, trying to thrust her suspicions to the back of her mind, but when she looked out from beneath the thick fringe of her lashes and saw Delia possessively squeezing Jared's arm, suspicion surged forth again, stronger now. Horrified by the mere possibility that her father was being betrayed, she was nearly overcome by a debilitating weariness. Her skin grew clammy; she swayed slightly. Jared immediately disentangled himself from Delia's clinging hands and one long stride brought him close to Suzanne. When one large hand lightly cupped her elbow, she suppressed the desire to jerk free of his gentle grasp and looked up at him, unaware of the tiredness and vulnerability that darkened her wide green eyes.

"Are you feeling all right, Miss Collins?" he asked,

his tone slightly warmer now. "Would you like to sit down and rest a moment?"

Shaking her head, she swallowed with some difficulty. Having never been this close to him before, she hadn't realized how tall he was. She was nearly five-foot-four herself but he seemed at least a foot taller and in no way slight of build, muscular, though certainly not burly. There was a subtle strength conveyed by his long lean body that she suddenly found infinitely disturbing. Her heartbeat quickened as her bemused gaze was captured by dark intelligent eyes that narrowed intently as he surveyed her upturned face. Unable to withstand that disconcerting eye contact, she swiftly looked away and fidgeted nervously with the buttons on the jacket of her powder blue suit.

"No, thank you, I don't need to sit down," she finally murmured. "I'm all right."

Jared's fingers tightened slightly around her upper arm. "I know you've been ill so . . ."

"I'm perfectly fine now," Suzanne insisted softly. "Really, I am."

"But you don't look fine, darling," Delia interceded, feigning great concern as she stepped forward and actually patted Suzanne's cheek. "You've gone a little pale. Hasn't she, Jared? See, her charming freckles are more noticeable now, don't you think? Why don't you sit down a minute, honey? I'm worried about you."

"Then I'll let you carry your own makeup again," Suzanne said tersely, retaliating to some extent for her stepmother's hypocrisy by thrusting the cosmetic case in her direction. "It's quite heavy."

As she glanced at the case, Delia's eyes took on a hard glitter but that vanished completely as she looked up at Jared and her hand fluttered out in a helpless little gesture. "Would you mind carrying that for me, darling?"

When he took the case from Suzanne, his fingers grazed hers but he didn't seem to notice. Instead his dark brows lifted and he smiled wryly at Delia. "She's right; it is heavy. What are you carrying in here? Bars of gold or rocks?"

Delia giggled foolishly and gave him one of her femme fatale smiles as she reached up to unnecessarily adjust his wine-colored tie. "You know how women are. We have to carry all our little jars and pots and bottles along with us everywhere we go. We'd be positively lost without all our creams and lotions to make us beautiful."

"And do you carry an entire cosmetic counter in your bag too, Miss Collins?" Jared inquired, slipping the strap of Suzanne's tote bag off her shoulder, despite her insistence that she could carry it herself. The canvas tote was considerably lighter than the red leather case and his brows lifted again. As a slight smile curved his firm yet sensuously shaped lips, amusement gentled his rugged features. "Obviously you didn't pack all your jars and pots and bottles in here. If you don't use lotions and creams, how do you account for your perfect skin?"

"Oh, she's the outdoorsy type," Delia spoke up, her smile insincere. "What I've never understood is why she doesn't always have a tan since she stays out so much. But I guess that's because you redheads have such sensitive skin, don't you, dear? You never can get a deep tan, can you? Pity."

A biting retort sprang to Suzanne's lips but she suppressed it, refusing to indulge in a verbal sparring with Delia about a subject as unimportant as a suntan. Besides, she was beginning to feel rather exhausted. The flight had been long and her shoulders drooped slightly as she glanced at her wristwatch and found it was half past midnight. Her eyes held a hint of appeal as they sought Jared's face.

"We'll leave for the hotel as soon as I retrieve your luggage," he responded perceptively, his own dark gaze narrowing. "I'll take your luggage claim checks and both of you can sit down and wait here for me."

Happy to comply, Suzanne gave him two baggage checks then settled herself in one of a seemingly endless row of plastic molded seats. Though Delia poised herself prettily on the chair beside her, they pointedly ignored each other for the next ten minutes. When Jared returned with a porter pushing a cart containing Delia's five red suitcases and Suzanne's two, they all went out of the terminal into the cool night air. Moonless, the sky was like black velvet, scattered with twinkling stars. Away from the noisy hustle and bustle inside the building, Suzanne felt less tired as she waited with Delia for Jared to bring his car around and pick them up. When he parked the cream-colored Fiat Ritmo in front of them a few minutes later, the porter soon discovered all the luggage wouldn't fit into the back of the car. Delia quickly swept past her step-daughter to claim the front passenger seat so Suzanne found herself relegated to the back seat along with three red crushed leather suitcases.

"Sorry you're so squeezed in back there," Jared remarked as he slid into the driver's seat. Glancing back over his shoulder, he gave her a wry smile as she shifted around, trying to find a comfortable position. "I would have hired a truck if I'd realized Delia traveled with enough luggage to see her through a year-long cruise around the world. I'm glad to see you didn't follow her example."

Even that very impersonal compliment didn't sit well with Delia. As if she felt Jared was affording Suzanne too much attention, she leaned toward him, stretching a silk-clad arm across the back of the driver's seat. She pursed her lips into an exaggerated little pout that Suzanne found particularly irritating. And when her stepmother began talking too quietly for her to hear, effectively excluding her from the conversation, Suzanne turned her head to gaze out the window. Ahead, Rome was a black silhouette etched on a background of purplish black sky. Streetlights along the main thoroughfares shimmered like six-pointed stars guiding them into the city.

Despite the late hour, traffic was quite heavy. When Jared exited the modern autostrada and expertly maneuvered the Ritmo into the jumbled flow of vehicles on one of the city's older streets, Suzanne easily recognized why traffic mishaps were legend here. Almost everyone seemed to drive in a chaotic willy-nilly fashion. Cars darted in and out of the unorderly flow and though Suzanne imagined she would panic if forced to drive in such crazy traffic, Jared didn't act as if it bothered him one whit. One lean hand controlled the wheel and his posture was relaxed, despite the fact that a taxi nearly hit them and Delia was chattering like a magpie all the while besides.

To Suzanne's relief, they soon turned onto a less congested street, passed over the dark ribbon of the Tiber River, then wound their way through the city to the Via Veneto, the avenue on which the hotel was located. Along the way, Suzanne caught glimpses inside dimly lighted nightclubs and discotheques as patrons opened the doors to exit or enter. As tired as she was at the moment, she couldn't imagine being energetic enough to go dancing so late. So she was glad when Jared at last pulled over to the curb by a canopied walkway before a gray stone building. A doorman, resplendent in a scarlet uniform complete with tasseled epaulets, ushered them from the car and into the lobby while a bellman struggled with Delia's luggage.

Inside the scarlet carpeted lobby were marble busts of Roman emperors and life size statues of their gods and goddesses tucked away in recessed nooks at intervals along the tiled walls. Obviously an expensive old hotel, the decor was opulent but not in the least bit tacky. Yet Suzanne only vaguely recognized the atmosphere of aesthetic splendor. Her head was beginning to feel too heavy on her slender neck and, unable to bite back a yawn, she hid it behind her hand. A faint unreasonable blush crept into her cheeks as Jared finished at the registration desk, turned, and smiled almost indulgently just as her yawn was ending. With his coat and vest unbuttoned now and his tie loosened, he seemed more approachable. She returned his smile hesitantly but as he started walking in her direction, Delia intercepted him. So once again, Suzanne trailed along behind them as they followed the sleepy-eyed bellman onto a quaint grill-doored elevator.

After a somewhat jerky ascent to the third floor, Jared indicated with a gesture that both Delia and Suzanne precede him along a dimly lighted narrow corridor. The bellman stopped at Delia's room first and as he unlocked the door then began carrying all her paraphernalia inside, she stretched up on tiptoe to kiss Jared's cheek and smiled provocatively at him. That smile faded, however, as she turned to Suzanne though her tone of voice was sugary sweet. "Good night, dear. Do try to go right to sleep so you won't feel worn out tomorrow. And . . . uh . . . I never rest well in a hotel so . . . don't disturb me during the night, please, because I'll never get back to sleep."

An odd request, Suzanne thought, frowning slightly. "I had no intention of disturbing you," she said tonelessly. "Why should I want to do that?"

Without answering, Delia smiled again at Jared then slowly ambled into her room. As she closed the door behind her, Jared escorted Suzanne across the hall and three doors down. As the bellman took her canvas suitcases inside, she impulsively extended her hand then mentally berated herself for trembling slightly as his fingers grazed her palm as he took it. "Thank you for meeting us at the airport," she said, her words rushed and rather self-conscious. "You've been very helpful, very kind."

Then, though she tried to extract her hand from his, he didn't release her. Catching her surprised look, his black eyes impaled the luminous green depths of hers. "Why do you dislike Delia?" he asked abruptly. "Do you resent her for marrying Jack?"

"Resent her? No, I don't think I resent her," Suzanne answered stiffly. "I . . . we just don't have much in common, I guess."

"She married your father." Flicking back the front of his coat, Jared slid long fingers into his left trouser pocket. "So the two of you have Jack in common."

"But I rarely see either of them."

"Whose fault is that?"

"I wasn't aware that it was anyone's *fault,*" she muttered, running her fingers through the tumbled cascade of russet hair pulled back from her face. "Somehow it's just happened that we don't see each other often. But I don't think I dislike Delia. She's simply not at all like my mother and I can't . . . relate to her."

"You should try to during this visit," Jared declared firmly, as if he were issuing a command rather than a request. "Jack's heart attack was mild but he shouldn't be subjected to any unwarranted tension. And if you're antagonistic toward Delia, he'll be upset. So try to be pleasant, for his sake."

Suddenly resentment surpassed Suzanne's weariness. Emerald eyes glimmered with indignation. "I happen to know how to behave, Mr. Caine, so I don't need you giving me instructions. I wouldn't upset Dad. If I didn't care about the state of his health, why would I have wanted to visit him in the first place?"

"Wanted to?" Jared repeated somewhat mockingly then lifted a silencing hand as she started to speak. Surveying her thoroughly, from her small slender feet in brown kid pumps to the fiery hair framing her small face, he shook his head. "We'll continue this discussion later. Right now, you need sleep. If you're feeling exceedingly tired, I'll postpone our 9:00 A.M. flight and we'll take the afternoon plane to Milan. Would you like for me to do that?"

Confused by his abrupt switch from behavioral advisor to concerned protector, she frowned slightly but shook her head. "No. Don't postpone the flight on my account. Nine o'clock won't be too early for me. I don't usually need a lot of sleep," she exaggerated just a bit. Actually, at the moment, she felt as if she could go into hibernation for a month and still awaken in need of more rest, but she didn't want to admit that to him for some reason. Perhaps subconsciously reluctant to show him any sign of weakness, she squared her shoulders. "Nine o'clock will be fine because I'm feeling perfectly well now, really."

"If you say so," was his disturbing answer as he inclined his dark head then started to turn and walk away toward the door next to Delia's where the bellman waited.

A compulsion in Suzanne made her reach out and touch his arm but she pulled her hand back immediately as she felt his muscles go taut beneath her fingers. She gestured rather nervously. "I . . . well, thanks for offering to postpone the flight though," she blurted out. "It was kind of you to consider it since I'm sure you need to get back to Como as soon as possible. You must be extremely busy reorganizing the new silk firm you and Dad bought."

"Some things are more important than business," he replied very seriously. "During the two years we've been based in Como, I've learned that schedules should be broken occasionally. The accurate time is of little concern to most of the people who live there and they're much less tense because of their attitude. There's a lot to be said for controlling time rather than letting it control you so I wouldn't mind at all postponing the flight tomorrow. Now, do you want me to?"

She shook her head again. "No. Dad will be expecting us earlier. I don't want to disappoint him."

"Then I suggest you get some sleep." Jared said as he walked away. "Good night, Miss Collins."

After murmuring good night to him, Suzanne went into her room, quickly shed her clothes and took a fast shower. After donning a green cotton nightgown, she haphazardly brushed her hair, then climbed into bed without any more undue ceremony. It felt so nice to stretch out on the cool sheets but even as she nuzzled her cheek against the plump pillow, she was remembering Delia's request that she not disturb her during the night. Why had she found it necessary to say that? It didn't make much sense . . . unless Delia planned to share her bed tonight with Jared and of course wanted to make certain her stepdaughter didn't accidentally find them together. The possibility was too upsetting to contemplate. Yet, tired as she was, Suzanne couldn't seem to dismiss it. Had Delia and Jared planned this rendezvous and was that why she had tried to discourage Suzanne from coming to Italy? And what had Jared meant when he said some things were more important than business? What things? Delia? And the opportunity to spend tonight with her in Rome, far from the people in Como who would know them?

Or maybe she was simply unduly suspicious of Delia, Suzanne reasoned as she turned restlessly in her bed. Jared Caine could be a kind considerate man. She had seen some evidence of that tonight so surely he wouldn't think of having an affair with his partner's wife. Or would he? Suzanne had no way to judge the kind of man he might be since she barely knew him.

With such thoughts buzzing in her head, she expected to spend a restless night. Yet, she was exhausted from the long flight and the lingering effects of the brief but intense illness, and she curled up in the center of the bed like a drowsy little kitten, hugged her pillow to her and fell asleep. But she dreamed repeatedly of Delia's clinging hands on Jared's arm and of his tanned face and the piercing look in his dark eyes that defied analysis.

Chapter Three

The flight to Milan the next morning was pleasantly short. Compared to the journey the day before, this one seemed a long ascent and descent with little time spent flying at a level high altitude. Consequently, Suzanne didn't feel at all tired when they landed at the airport and immediately left for Como in Jared's silver Jaguar XJ6. A sedan, the car could accommodate all of Delia's luggage without Suzanne having to share the backseat with any of it. Running her hand appreciatively over the rich black leather upholstery, she settled herself to enjoy the sights along the super autostrada they would follow to Como, nestled in the foothills of Lombardy's lake district.

As Delia's audible but indiscernible nonstop chatter wafted back from the front seat, Suzanne tuned it out deliberately, not wanting to try to imagine what her stepmother was saying to Jared Caine. Last night's dreams hadn't allayed her suspicions about the two of them. In fact, she had awakened that morning wondering what an intelligent man like Jared could ever see in a shallow female like Delia. But then, she had often wondered what her father had seen in her. He too was an intelligent man but he had married Delia! Perhaps there was a certain charm about silly women like her stepmother that men responded to but which remained an undecipherable mystery to other women. Perhaps there was, but Suzanne seriously doubted it. What could be charming and alluring about someone who tittered constantly and who never allowed herself to be real? Delia's life's work was putting on a pretense designed specifically to ensnare men and Suzanne couldn't imagine why her father and Jared didn't see her for the fraud that she was. Yet, they didn't and, realizing she could do nothing to open their eyes to Delia's faults, Suzanne resolved not to let the situation bother her unduly. Forcing herself to ignore the fact that her stepmother was sitting as close to Jared as the bucket seat and gear console would allow, she turned her attention to the tumbling foothills sloping up before them.

Within thirty minutes after leaving Milan, they reached Como. Although an industrial as well as resort town, it had retained a pristine beauty as it spread out around the tip of the long, narrow, three-pronged lake. As Jared drove down a busy tree-lined avenue, Suzanne admired the cream-colored buildings with their coral-hued tile roofs. But it was the lake they were approaching that she always found breathtakingly beautiful. She had visited her father twice before since he had moved here; yet once again she was nearly mesmerized by Lake Como's loveliness.

Sapphire water sparkled at the foot of the rolling green hills that stairstepped up in terraced vineyards and hayfields and were dotted with small farms and gleaming villas. Greenery carpeted the entire lake basin with a nearly Mediterrean-like lushness that was delightfully unexpected, considering the fact that the snow-tipped Alps towered in the distance. When they had left the city behind a few minutes later and Jared turned onto a narrower winding road that ascended and bisected the rolling hills, Suzanne looked down on the lake. Small boats with white triangular sails glided across the azure water, only infinitesimally disturbing the placid surface set ashimmer by golden sunlight. Despite Delia, despite her lack of a really close relationship with her father, Suzanne loved it here. Though the mountains of Vermont possessed an unrivaled beauty, the loveliness of Lake Como was different, more exotic. Everything about the area appealed to her innermost romantic nature and seemed to awaken her senses to a keener awareness. The air smelled fresher. The sky looked a deeper clearer blue. Or maybe she was simply being fanciful, she considered, breathing a soft sigh.

At the barely audible sound, Jared glanced back at her over his shoulder. "Did something specific cause that sigh or was it just an expression of your feelings for everything in general?" he asked while turning his eyes to the tortuously winding road again. "Or are you feeling tired?"

"Oh, no. I'm fine," Suzanne hastened to assure him, ignoring the irritated glance Delia shot back at her. "I was just thinking how beautiful it is here. There's something so alluring, almost enchanting . . . oh, well, I'm sure you don't need me to tell you how lovely Lake Como is, since you live here. Are you still in an apartment in town, Mr. Caine, or have you rented a villa since I was here last time?"

"He *bought* a villa several months ago," Delia announced smugly, as if taking some credit for his purchase. Apparently unwilling to be excluded from the conversation, she patted her sleek black hair and gave her stepdaughter a patently false smile as she continued, "You should see it, dear. It's larger than our villa and much more elegant, I think. Or at least it will be when it's been completely redecorated. And Jared's about to give me a free hand as far as that's concerned. Aren't you, Jared?"

He glanced at her, his brows lifting as if this was the first he had heard of such a suggestion. Yet, if it was, he was too polite to say so. He simply shrugged. "I like the villa the way it is," he answered, either not noticing or not caring that Delia's features hardened with impatience. "So what would be the point of redecorating?"

"But, darling, aren't you just getting sick of all those tapestry covered sofas and chairs and all that heavy mahogany inlaid with ivory? And those marble floors look too bare, too cold. The woven rugs scattered here and there don't help much and they're so old-fashioned." Smiling beguilingly, she stroked the broadcloth sleeve of his gray suit coat. "Everything's too old-fashioned. You really need to lighten the atmosphere."

"How? With chrome and glass and white sectional sofas?" he responded wryly. "No thanks. If I had wanted to live in surroundings like that, I would have stayed in my apartment. A villa should look like a villa and the spacious rooms allow for what you call a 'heavy decor.'"

"But, Jared, I think. . . ."

"Since we can't agree on that, maybe we need a third opinion," he continued, unperturbed. "Suzanne can take a look at the villa and tell us what she thinks. I would imagine she has some inherent sense of what is and isn't appropriate since Jack told me she's an art major." Glancing toward the backseat, he smiled slightly. "By any chance, have you steered yourself toward a career in interior design, Suzanne?"

Something about the low lazy cadence of his voice saying her name made her heart palpitate oddly for several seconds. After gazing with some fascination at the strong brown column of his neck rising above his white shirt collar for an indeterminate time, she at last roused herself sufficiently to shake her head. "Well, no . . . I . . . actually, I haven't decided exactly what kind of career I want."

"Really, dear? Well, don't you think you should be making a decision soon? After all, you'll be a senior before you know it," Delia contributed inanely, then giggled. "And you don't want to become one of those perpetual students who make going to school forever a career, do you?"

Detecting the underlying cattiness in Delia's tone, Suzanne ignored her remark altogether, not that her lack of response mattered. Never one to appreciate occasional lapses of silence, Delia began chattering again to Jared, this time relating choice bits of gossip about mutal acquaintances. Though she barely paused for breath during her monologue, he didn't really appear to be listening, Suzanne noticed with some satisfaction.

She sat up straighter in her seat a minute or so later when Jared swung the Jaguar off the narrow road onto a drive lined by tall tapered Lombardy poplars that swayed in a gentle breeze. Beyond a bend stood the villa, a beige structure, relatively unadorned except for the wrought iron railings along the upper floor balconies, but the lushly green grounds scattered with pine trees enhanced the simple lines of the house. As Jared stopped the car on the circle drive before the front portico, Lucia, the housekeeper, hurried out of the house, smoothing work-roughened hands over the skirt of her black uniform. She bestowed a warm smile on Jared as he got out of the car, then gave a more cautious one to Delia after he came around to help her out. And as he opened Suzanne's door and she stood on the pebbled drive, she noticed that the housekeeper seemed almost visibly relieved. She soon knew why.

"Oh, *signorina,* you look well," Lucia said enthusiastically. "Signore Collins will be happy that you are not so ill as he feared. He has—"

"Find Carlo and carry this luggage inside immediately," Delia interrupted imperiously. "I don't want all my clothes to be wrinkled so have them unpacked before you serve lunch." As the housekeeper nodded resignedly and rushed away, perfectly manicured fingers fluttered up to rest lightly on Jared's shoulder. "You will join us for lunch, won't you?" she breathed, her voice now husky as she reverted back to her weak and helpless little woman routine. Gazing up from beneath eyelashes too long to be real, she smiled seductively. "Please do stay."

To Suzanne's surprise, he shook his head. "Thanks, but I really should go."

"Oh, but you have to stay," Delia persisted rather childishly. "If you don't, I won't have anyone to talk to. You know Jack will give all his attention to Suzanne because it's been so long since he's seen her."

Doubting that very much, Suzanne started to turn away but at that instant, her eyes met Jared's dark piercing gaze and she could almost imagine he knew what she was thinking. Yet how could he possibly know that she felt as if her father had become a stranger after her mother had died? The vague resentment she felt because he had shut her out of his life at a time when she had needed him badly was an emotion she always made a concerted effort to conceal. So unless Jared Caine was a mind reader or else amazingly perceptive, he couldn't recognize her feelings. Yet those black eyes seemed capable of discerning her innermost emotions; caught by his mesmerizingly intense gaze, she was rooted to the spot where she stood for a moment that lasted an eternity. At last his probing survey of her ceased and she was able to breathe deeply again, though her confusion about him doubled when he abruptly changed his mind about the luncheon invitation.

"All right, I think I will stay," he acquiesced, gently removing the clinging hand from his and holding it only for an instant before releasing it. He smiled at Delia. "I would like to talk to Jack if he's feeling up to it."

"Oh, I'm sure he'll want to see you too. You know how he is. He'll have to know all the details of your business trip to Rome," Delia bubbled over, Little Miss Sunshine now that she had gotten what she wanted. Curling her hand possessively around Jared's arm, she started walking across the tiled portico and it was only as an afterthought that she glanced back over her shoulder at Suzanne who was following at a respectful ten paces. "Jack's waiting so don't dawdle, dear."

Don't dawdle, dear, Suzanne mimicked uncharitably beneath her breath, a frown knitting her brow as her stepmother clung even more tenaciously to Jared's arm. To his credit, he didn't seem to actively encourage Delia's proprietorial attitude toward him but Suzanne had to wonder if he was merely being discreet. Yet, she was also somewhat ashamed of this suspicious side of her nature that she had never known she possessed until last night. Though she had no confidence whatsoever in Delia's sense of morality, she wanted very much to believe that Jared's moral standards wouldn't allow him to have an affair with another man's wife. Yet she had no idea why she felt this incongruously strong need to believe in him and, wearying of this futile attempt at self-analysis, she tried to focus her mind on something else.

As it happened, all her previous thoughts *were* temporarily suspended when she followed Jared and her stepmother into the villa's main hall. Halting abruptly, she stared around her in amazement, feeling as if she had walked into a place she had never seen before. Since her last visit, Delia had been very busy and had managed to obliterate nearly every sign that this house was indeed an Italian villa. The lovely tile floor was now covered wall to wall with white plush carpeting as were the marble stairs that led up to the second floor. The heavy bronze lamps that had been mounted on the walls were now replaced with frivolous crystal light fixtures with ridiculous teardrop prisms dangling from them. In some ways, Suzanne was a purist and she agreed with Jared that a villa should look like a villa but, judging by this main hall, Delia didn't agree with them. Unwilling to show her distaste for the new decor, she tried to maintain a noncommittal expression as she followed the white carpeting extending into the salon. What she saw was disappointing. The beautiful frescoed walls had been covered by expensive white linen panels and the white sectional sofa Jared had mentioned formed a conversation area along with two royal blue overstuffed modern chairs. Chrome and glass tables abounded but luckily the starkness of it all was relieved by paintings done in vibrant colors, original bronze objets d'art, and several exquisite Ming dynasty vases. As a whole, the affluent decor was balanced and tastefully done but was far more appropriate for a penthouse in Rome than for a villa overlooking Lake Como. Distressed especially by the loss of the fading but still beautifully unique wall frescoes, Suzanne was unable to make any comment.

Delia, however, found her silence unacceptable. "Well, what do you think?" she prompted. "Do you like it?"

Since this was Delia's house, the choosing of a decor was strictly her business and Suzanne knew an expression of her true feelings wouldn't be appreciated. "It's nice. Very modern," she answered discreetly, her gaze wandering involuntarily to Jared. Suspecting she saw a glimmer of understanding in his dark eyes and wondering again if he could possibly know what she was thinking, she blushed and decided a hasty retreat was in order. Forcing a smile for her stepmother, she uttered an evasive truth. "You did a great job of coordinating everything."

Delia's perfectly arched brows lifted slightly, as if she hadn't expected a compliment but she recovered from her surprise quickly and shot Jared a smug smile. "Well, now, since Suzanne approves of what I've done here, you can trust me to redecorate your villa, can't you?"

Still looking at Suzanne, he obviously caught the pained expression that flickered across her face because an oddly indulgent smile etched deep creases into his lean cheeks. Yet, he must not have been perversely amused that she had been placed in such an uncomfortable position because he provided her with a means of escape. "I think Suzanne should get a chance to see my villa before she makes any decision," he told Delia. "Besides, she doesn't want to think about decors right now. She's anxious to see Jack, I'm sure."

"Oh, yes, I am," Suzanne agreed swiftly, giving him a rather shy smile of gratitude before looking at Delia again. "Could I see Dad now? Or do you think he's resting?"

"I'm sure he isn't if Lucia has run and told him you're here," Delia responded, something like resentment in her sharp tone. With an impatient toss of her hand indicating Suzanne should follow, she marched out of the salon. "Come on then, I might as well go up with you and say hello to him. But I won't be long, Jared, so don't run away."

He didn't answer but as Suzanne walked past him on her way out of the salon, he caught her bare upper arm in a light yet firm grip, halting her steps. "Try not to look so nervous," he advised softly, his eyes darkening to black as they swept over the delicate features of her face. "Jack is your father. You shouldn't dread seeing him."

"But I don't . . ." she began until the disconcerting intensity of his gaze prevented her from uttering the untruth she had started to tell. The edge of her small white even teeth pressed down into the soft curve of her lower lip and she breathed a sigh. "All right, maybe I am a a little nervous. But you can't possibly understand how I feel."

"I'd like to try," Jared said, his voice lowering to a near whisper. "Maybe we could talk about it."

"Why should you care about my feelings?" Suzanne blurted our confusedly. "I don't understand your interest."

"Jack's my friend," he answered simply. "And he—"

"Are you coming any time soon, Suzanne?" Delia snapped irritably from the foot of the carpeted stairs where she stood, tapping her toe with ill-concealed impatience. "Your father's waiting, I'm sure. So say whatever you have to say to Jared later."

"We *will* discuss this later," Jared promised, his fingertips trailing across the sensitive skin of her arm as he slowly released her. As a slight tremor shook her body with the unintentional caress, his eyes narrowed. Suddenly his jaw tightened; his expression became almost indifferent as he thrust his hands into his trouser pockets and inclined his head in Delia's direction. "Go ahead. You don't want to keep Jack waiting."

Thoroughly perplexed by the strange conversation, Suzanne glanced back over her shoulder with a puzzled frown as she crossed the hall, but Jared was no longer standing in the doorway of the salon. Shaking her head thoughtfully, she trailed her hand along the wrought iron bannister as she ascended the stairs, then stopped short when she nearly ran over Delia, who was waiting on the landing, hands planted firmly on her hips.

"You're wasting your time trying to cozy up to Jared," the older woman declared with a toss of her head. "I know you find him attractive—I've never met a woman who didn't—but you'll just make a fool of yourself if you decide to pursue him. He's a sophisticated man. He'll never be interested in an adolescent like you. I just thought I should tell you that for your own good."

"Thanks for your concern," Suzanne retorted with some sarcasm. "But I don't happen to have any plans to pursue Mr. Caine so I don't need your advice. And I don't consider myself an adolescent. I'll be twenty-one next month."

"But you'll still look fourteen," Delia shot back maliciously. "You're hardly what I'd call a sophisticate and I'm just warning you that Jared's only interested in sophisticated women."

Though Suzanne curled her hands into tight little fists at her side, she refused to be provoked into an all-out battle of words with her stepmother before she had even had a chance to see her father. "Yes. Well, fine, I'll consider myself forewarned that Mr. Caine's only interested in sophisticated women, not that I care much one way or another. Now if that satisfies you, could I see Dad?"

"But of course, dear," Delia replied, supreme satisfaction glittering in her eyes. "I only wanted to make certain we understand each other. Now that we do, let's not keep Jack waiting any longer."

Mentally counting to ten, Suzanne followed as the older woman slowly sauntered down the hall, then swept open the third door on the left without knocking and glided into the room. Suzanne was not so brash.

Stopping hesitantly in the doorway, she looked immediately toward the bed but her father wasn't there, as she had fully expected him to be. Instead, he was sitting up in an easy chair by the French doors that opened onto the balcony. His hair was a little grayer and the lines in his face had deepened slightly but, except for those inevitable signs of aging, he hadn't changed much since she had seen him last, nearly eight months ago. As usual there was an aura of virility about him that even a minor heart seizure hadn't diminished. And, rather than being clad in pajamas and robe, he was dressed in casual navy slacks and a white polo shirt. Smiling a welcome, he held out one hand to his daughter but before Suzanne could advance one step into the room, Delia descended on him. "What are you doing out of bed, Jack?" she fussed, hands all aflutter. "You're not supposed to be sitting up yet. Before I left for the States, the doctor said you needed to stay in bed at least another week!"

"I know more about what's right for me than any doctor," Jack Collins declared firmly, catching one of his wife's gesticulating hands. Pulling her down so her face was level with his, he pressed a brief kiss against her lips but that silenced her only momentarily.

"Really, Jack," she chided, straightening again and smoothing her hair though it was still arranged perfectly. "You're the most impossible man. I've only been gone three days and I don't like coming back to find you disobeying the doctor's orders. I don't think I could stand it if you had another attack, so please . . ."

"Stop clucking over me like an old mother hen," Jack commanded, then laughed up at her indulgently as she stamped one foot in frustration. "You should know me well enough by now not to be surprised to find me out of bed. Lying there day after day was driving me crazy. So I decided that kind of tension was worse for my heart than getting up and sitting in this chair. Now, stop trying to treat me like a helpless invalid."

"But Jack," Delia whined. "I. . . ."

"You're not going to change my mind," her husband said, setting his jaw determinedly. "Now, be quiet a minute while I say hello to Suzanne."

Astoundingly, Delia obeyed, though with a disapproving sniff and a genuine pout pursing her lips as Suzanne walked quickly across the room to take her father's hand. Bending down, she kissed his cheek. "Hello, Dad," she murmured too shyly, emotion causing a little catch in her voice. Straightening, she smiled down at him. "How are you feeling?"

"Cranky. Sick of being stuck in this room," he retorted, though he suddenly seemed less relaxed than he had been when talking to Delia. His expression almost seemed to harden as he examined Suzanne carefully but he patted her hand before releasing it, then looked her over again. "But never mind about me. How are you feeling? It was upsetting to hear you were in the hospital. I've been worried."

"I'm fine now. I just didn't get enough rest during exams so I couldn't shake off the cold I caught."

Jack frowned. "Pneumonia is a little more serious than you're making it sound, isn't it?"

"I'm going back downstairs," Delia spoke up sharply, probably perturbed that she wasn't getting much attention. "You two can have a nice chat until lunch and I'll entertain Jared."

"Jared's still here?" Jack questioned. "Good. I want to talk to him about his Rome trip."

"After lunch, darling, if you're not too tired," Delia said too sweetly as she reached the doorway and turned to blow him a kiss. "You just concern yourself with catching up on all Suzanne's news. I'll take very good care of Jared."

I bet you will, Suzanne thought uncharitably, suspicion rising anew though she tried to thrust concern for her father to the back of her mind. Judging by the way he had handled Delia a few moments ago, he could easily take care of himself and didn't need his daughter fretting about him. Still, she couldn't help hoping desperately that she was mistaken in her fear that Delia and Jared might be having an affair. Perhaps the fact that she and her stepmother had never exactly been wild about each other made her overly suspicious. Needing to believe that, she had almost convinced herself it was true by the time Delia blew Jack another kiss, then hurried away to go play hostess for Jared.

With father and daughter left alone in the bedroom, an uncomfortable silence commenced. Uncertain of how to initiate a conversation, Suzanne glanced around, dismayed that the redecoration project had extended even up here. At least the carpet wasn't white; it was a very pale blue but all the furniture was light pecan and of a Scandinavian, somewhat modular, design, that seemed inappropriate for a mellow old villa.

"Well, sit down, honey, and let's talk," Jack finally spoke, after clearing his throat uneasily. "Pull that vanity chair over here and tell me about school."

"There's not much to tell actually," Suzanne said, settling herself on the blue velvet cushion of the vanity seat a moment later. "You know, Lynn and I go to our classes, study, or just loaf around sometimes. Nothing really changes much from semester to semester." As she idly twisted the strap of her purse around her fingers, her eyes suddenly brightened to emerald. "Oh, but when you wrote to me about buying the silk firm here, you did pique my interest so I took a course in fabric design. We did some screen printing."

"I never knew you were interested in any of my business ventures," her father said with a rather pleased smile. "I imagined girls your age would find the world of commerce dry and unexciting."

Suzanne laughed softly. "Well, I have to admit some of the companies you buy don't exactly thrill me. I mean, when you got into manufacturing machine parts, I didn't run out and sign up for a course in tool and dye making. But silk is different."

"More romantic?" Jack Collins said wryly. "Well, I suppose it would appeal to you more than machine parts. Since you're interested, you'll have to tour the mill in Como while you're here."

"Oh, I'd like that if you're sure I wouldn't get in anyone's way." Feeling more relaxed now, she positioned herself more comfortably on the velvet-cushioned seat. "So. Has the mill turned out to be another great success for Collins-Caine Enterprises?"

"Profits are increasing. It was a family-operated business, started by Renato Gallio about seventy years ago but the latest generation of sons wasn't particularly interested in keeping it going. One became a professional soccer player and the other didn't want to devote his every waking moment to the mill so they sold us controlling interest. Jared retained all the old employees and hired some new ones. He reorganized the entire operation and everything is running much more smoothly now."

Looking down, Suzanne unnecessarily brushed her hand over her navy blue skirt, then tugged at the cotton lace collar of her sleeveless white blouse. "Uh, about Jared—I guess I've never really known how he became your partner or why you even took on a partner at all, especially one so young."

"Oh, I simply got tired of carrying all the responsibility," Jack explained, stroking his chin. "A friend of mine in San Francisco introduced me to Jared. He'd made money on some very shrewd investments and he brought that into the partnership along with some very innovative ideas. He's an exceptional businessman, seems to have some sixth sense about which deals to make and which ones to steer clear of. And his reorganization of the firms we buy never fails to increase profits considerably."

"You make him sound perfect," Suzanne said doubtingly. "What makes his reorganizing methods so terrific?"

"Common sense," Jack replied flatly, lighting a cigarette despite her disapproving look. After inhaling deeply, he shrugged. "It's simple, really. For example, at the silk mill, Jared made Vito Gallio manager, so we could retain the atmosphere of a family-run business. Vito has responsibilities but they don't take up his entire life, which is what he wanted to avoid. More importantly, though, Jared believes in involving the employees in the operation. He listens to their ideas. He even divides them into groups, and each group is responsible for a product from start to finish. They feel more of a sense of accomplishment that way. The people who operate the looms take more pride in their work when they see they're part of the group that designs the print, prints it, and fashions it into say, scarves. Like I said, Jared's methods are merely common sense, but it's a common sense few other manufacturers practice."

"I see," Suzanne murmured, more impressed now by Jared than she really wanted to be. Some vague intuition in her told her she should remain indifferent to him so she didn't really want to hear that he was an intelligent, perceptive person. Almost wishing she hadn't questioned her father about him, she stared down at the straw purse on her lap, her silky hair falling forward like a russet curtain to conceal her cheeks. "Well, I'm glad to hear business is going so well."

For a long moment, Jack Collins didn't answer. Then he cleared his throat again but even so, his voice was unusually husky when he finally spoke, "With every year that passes, you look more like your mother."

Suzanne's eyes darted up to meet his. This was the first time in years he had mentioned her mother. "You really think I look like her?" she asked softly, wistfully. And when he nodded a smile trembled on her lips. "That makes me happy. I always thought she was the most beautiful woman in the world but I guess most children think that about their mothers."

"But Katherine was beautiful and you are too," her father said with quiet assurance. But as he gazed out into space, resignation tightened his lips to a grim line.

Despite the compliment he had given her, Suzanne felt the moment of closeness they had shared vanish as quickly as it had come. Saddened that he had drawn away from her again, she breathed a silent sigh and ran her fingers through her hair. Not knowing what to say to him now, she was actually relieved when Delia suddenly glided into the room, the silk of her scarlet dress swirling prettily around her legs. After glancing at her stepdaughter, she smiled at her husband and, incredibly, the smile seemed genuine. "I've told Lucia to bring Suzanne's lunch up here with yours so you won't have to eat alone, darling."

"I have no intention of eating alone or of eating up here for that matter," Jack said, slowly rising to his feet. "No more meals up here in this room. From now on, I'm going downstairs to eat."

"But, Jack, the doctor will have a fit!" Delia cried. "You're not even supposed to be up and dressed. So he certainly won't like it if you try walking up and down those stairs. It's insanity! What are you trying to do? Have another attack?"

"Stop your fussing," he chided gently, going to lay one arm across her shoulders. "There. I'll lean on you if it'll make you feel any better."

"It won't! The only thing that will make me feel better is for you to go back to bed."

"And I refuse. I'm not going to overexert myself. Besides, I'd rather take my chances than stay in that bed," he announced bluntly, then looked at his daughter. "Don't you agree, Suzanne? It's better to take a few risks now and then than to be afraid to move. Right?"

Suzanne spread her hands in an uncertain gesture, not knowing what to say. Though she understood why he rebelled against staying in bed all the time, she didn't want to encourage him in something that might cause him to have another attack. So she said nothing and soon realized it really didn't matter. He had made his decision. He was going downstairs for lunch so nothing she might have said would have changed his mind anyhow.

In the dining room a few minutes later, Suzanne was seated across the table from Jared but he only smiled at her before turning his attention to Jack, who wanted to hear about his Rome trip. Since Lucia was cook as well as housekeeper, the meal was typically Italian, comprised of several courses, each one filling. The appetizer of paper-thin strips of succulent cured ham and iced melon balls was delicious, as was the fettuccine that followed. But by the time they finished the main dish, fish, freshly caught in the lake then broiled, Suzanne couldn't eat anything more. She politely declined the cheese, fruit and dessert courses and merely sipped her white Orvieto wine while the others finished.

After coffee in the salon, Jack Collins leaned forward in his chair. "If you're not in a rush to leave, Jared, I'd like to go over the May expenditures for the mill with you."

"Really, Jack, this is too much," Delia protested. "You should go lie down after being up all this time."

Casting her a withering glance that silenced her immediately, he shook his head. "You're trying to coddle me. I won't put up with it. I feel fine so if you and Suzanne will excuse us. . . ." Standing, he inclined his head toward Jared. "Let's go into the study."

After the men left, Delia rose to her feet with a sniff. "Well, even if he won't lie down, I'm going to. All these early morning flights have exhausted me. A nap might be refreshing." Glancing at her stepdaughter with an expression of bored indifference, she asked, "And you can entertain yourself, can't you, dear? You might even want to take a nap, too."

Suzanne shook her head. "I'd rather go for a walk outside."

"Suit yourself," Delia responded blithely as she sauntered to the door, then stopped momentarily. "On your way out, would you tell Lucia to awaken me before Jared leaves?"

Taking acquiescence for granted, the older woman disappeared into the hall before Suzanne could answer so she sought out Lucia in the kitchen. After delivering the message, Suzanne went outside through the back door. The housekeeper's husband, Pietro, who was the handyman, too, had a garden along the back stone path. The pungent scents of basil, rosemary, and numerous other herbs filled the air and there was a verdant patch of thriving tomato plants, scattered with drooping yellow blossoms.

It was a lovely day, awash with sunshine. Removing her navy espadrilles, Suzanne luxuriated in the feel of thick springy grass beneath her bare soles as she walked into a copse of juniper trees. The cooler air in the shade caressed her skin as she followed the sylvan path beneath the heavy boughs to a secluded bench, beyond sight of the villa. Last year, she had discovered it as a place for quiet contemplation and it was nice to visit it now. A few small twigs were scattered on the concrete bench and after brushing them away, she sat down. Leaning back on her hands, she lifted her face up to gaze at the blue patches of sky visible between the swaying upper branches of the trees.

She watched milk white clouds drift by overhead for several minutes, until at last a tremulous sigh escaped her lips as she recalled the fleeting moment of closeness she and her father had shared in his room before lunch. Why did he withdraw from her, she wondered bleakly. Unbidden memories of life the way it had been before her mother's death penetrated her consciousness and tears filled her eyes before she could prevent them. She rarely let herself think about the old days, but this time she was powerless to halt the resurgence of memories until a teardrop caught in the fringe of her lower lashes dropped onto her cheek and reminded her that she had to accept the reality of life as it was now. With an impatient swipe of her hand, she brushed the tear away, sat up straight, and opened her eyes.

She gasped softly as Jared sat down on the bench beside her, took a handkerchief from his pocket, and with the edge of the neatly folded square caught the last lingering tear that was sliding into the slight hollow of one cheek. Ignoring the entrancing rose color that bloomed beneath the surface of her creamy skin, he shed his suit coat and tie, making himself at once more approachable. Darkly mysterious eyes searched the soft green depths of hers with breathtaking intensity. "Need someone to talk to?" he asked, his low voice unexpectedly kind. "Care to tell me what the tears were for?"

Though she wanted to confide in him, she wasn't sure she should. Perhaps he was being nice to her now but she didn't really know him and often the most shallow people in the world could make a good impression for awhile. He could be one of them, though something deep inside her told her that he wasn't. Yet she didn't know how to go about telling him what had happened with her father so she simply shook her head. "Maybe I'm just tired from all the traveling."

"Maybe, but I don't think that's it. Something else is wrong. Are you pining for some special boyfriend who's waiting back in Vermont?"

"No, because there is no special boyfriend. Maybe I drank too much wine with lunch," she suggested, smiling tremulously. "That could have made me weepy."

"But it didn't. Can't you tell me the real reason you're upset? I'm a good listener."

She could only look up at him, suddenly too aware of his nearness. The white of his open collar accentuated the bronze tan of his smooth taut skin and she felt an insane need to slip her hands inside his unbuttoned vest, to run them lightly over the muscular contours of his chest, faintly discernible against the fabric of his shirt. Horrified at the erotic meanderings of her imagination, she blushed and bent her head. "I'm n-not really that upset," she lied unconvincingly. "I *am* just tired. Really."

"I don't believe you," he whispered, cupping her face in large gentle hands, lifting her chin so she had to look at him again. An enigmatic glow flared in the depths of his dark eyes. "But if you want to pretend to be tough and self-sufficient, I'll let you. This time."

Nearly mesmerized by the oddly uneven tenor of his

voice, she sat perfectly still until the rough cushion of his thumbs brushed over her high cheekbones then down across the soft full curving of her lips. Her breath caught. Her widening eyes became luminous pools of green as she recognized the promise flaming in his. As he moved closer, his muscular thigh touching hers, her heart began to thud with dizzying rapidity. Keen anticipation weakened her limbs as his thumb applied gentle pressure to her small chin, tugging her mouth open slightly and when he slowly lowered his dark head, her eyes fluttered shut. An exquisite, unfamiliar thrill quickened within her as his lips, warm and firm, touched hers as lightly as the caress of a breeze.

"Suzanne," he murmured, his kiss deepening with breathtaking swiftness. With her soft bemused sigh, his lips hardened and caught the tender lower curve of hers. But as her senses spiraled and she would have happily surrendered to the strong hands that spanned her waist and began to draw her to him, the moment was rudely interrupted.

"Do excuse me for disturbing this cozy little scene," Delia nearly snarled, mottled red flooding her face as both Jared and Suzanne turned to look at her. Her lips curled as she glowered at her stepdaughter, then turned her attention to Jared. "Lucia said you told her you had an appointment and couldn't wait to talk to me. Then she saw you walking down here. Seems to me you have plenty of time to waste."

As if he hadn't heard the snide comment, he glanced at his wristwatch, then at Suzanne. "I do have to go now."

Confused by the intense emotions his kiss had aroused, and dismayed that Delia had witnessed the kiss, Suzanne could only nod.

Jared's narrowed gaze swept over her, then he stood, picked up his coat, and tossed it over one shoulder.

"Sorry, Delia, I can't talk now. As you reminded me, I have an appointment and I'm late for it as it is," he said quite calmly as he walked past her. "But if it's important, you can call me tonight."

As he strode away through the copse of trees, Delia glared after him, then spun back to face Suzanne. "You don't listen very well, do you?" she asked furiously. "Didn't I tell you that you'd be a fool to chase after Jared? He may have kissed you but don't get the idiotic notion that he could ever be seriously interested in *you!*"

"I have no such ideas, I assure you," Suzanne responded as coolly as possible. "You're the one who's making too much of one little kiss, Delia, not me. Since I have been kissed before, it was no big deal."

"Being kissed by Jared is no big deal?" Delia hooted disbelievingly. "Oh, come on. I know better than that."

Every muscle in Suzanne's body tensed painfully as her face went slightly pale. She knew she should challenge Delia by asking her how she could possibly know anything about Jared's kissing but the words simply couldn't get past the sudden constriction in her throat. She swallowed with difficulty, knowing she wouldn't ask the question because she feared what the answer would be, and a nauseating heaviness dragged at her stomach as she watched her stepmother turn and stroll nonchalantly toward the villa.

Chapter Four

Delia gave a small dinner party the following Sunday night. Though Suzanne wondered if her father had recuperated long enough to begin socializing again, he insisted he wouldn't get overly tired if only a few people were invited. In this, Delia readily concurred, though she had a specific motive for keeping the party small, Suzanne realized as she went downstairs Sunday evening. In a soft forest green cotton jersey dress with a scooped scalloped neckline she felt feminine yet demure, unaware that the slightly clingy fabric of the fitted bodice and swing skirt hinted at the alluring curves of her slender body. Hesitating at the foot of the stairs, she touched the gold filigree barrettes that swept her auburn hair back from her temples, checking to make certain they were secure. Then, hearing voices in the salon, she walked across the hall and went in.

"Oh there you are, dear," Delia cried as joyously as if she had just spied a long lost friend. Taking the hand of the young man beside her, she pulled him with her as she hurried to where Suzanne stood. "Dear, this is Vito Gallio. Vito, Suzanne, Jack's daughter. She's come to visit for a few weeks but I think she's getting a little lonely. Maybe you'd like to show her some of the sights around Como."

It was such a blatant attempt at matchmaking that

Suzanne was mortified, though Vito graciously assured Delia that he would be delighted to agree to her suggestion. Despite the fact that he sounded truly sincere, Suzanne felt warm color suffuse her cheeks as she saw that Jared was watching from across the room. With him was a lovely young woman, in her late twenties perhaps, with thick raven hair and limpid brown eyes. As Suzanne was wondering who she was and if she had come to the party with him, Delia provided her with that information.

"Angelina, this is Suzanne," she cooed. "Suzanne, Angelina Sorveno. She's in charge of the print designers at the silk firm. You know, one of those sophisticated career girls."

It was a very unsubtle reminder that Jared preferred sophisticates and Suzanne got the message quite clearly. Refusing to satisfy her stepmother by responding to the baiting with even so much as an impatient glance, she simply smiled and inclined her head in greeting to the raven-haired woman. As Angelina smiled back, however, Suzanne could nearly feel Jared's gaze on her so she murmured a shy hello that elicited no response at all. He merely allowed his dark eyes to drift over her until every inch of her skin was burning. The tension he could always create in her tautened to such a degree that her palms were damp and her breathing was so shallow that she felt dizzy. Desperate to regain control her emotions, she hastily turned away from him and rushed across the room to the white velvet sofa where her father sat, sinking down beside him.

Delia didn't allow her to stay there long, however. With a swirl of her black chiffon skirt, she turned back to Vito with a coaxing smile. "Be a love, won't you and play bartender for me tonight, since Jack's not allowed to stay on his feet for long at a time?" When the young man nodded agreeably, she reached up to stroke his cheek and the pleated chiffon of her sleeve draped her upper arm attractively. Then she beckoned to Suzanne. "Come along, dear. You can help Vito serve the drinks. Angelina, Jared, do sit down on the love seat and relax. Tell Vito what you'd like to drink."

Although she knew she was being manipulated, Suzanne stood and followed Vito to the built-in bar across the room but she wondered how he felt about having her foisted on him for the entire evening. Actually, he didn't seem to mind. He looked her over with an appreciative smile and his voice was low as he said in stilted English. "I almost did not accept your stepmother's invitation to dinner tonight. But now that I have met you, *signorina,* I am very glad that I did accept."

"Thank you," Suzanne murmured. "You're very kind to say that."

"Kind?" Vito exclaimed softly, twisting his mouth into a comical grimace, as he shook his head emphatically. "I am Italian and Italian men do not compliment women to be kind. We compliment them because they are so feminine and beautiful. And that is why I complimented you."

Suzanne had to laugh at such outrageous flattery and when Vito joined in her laughter, some of the tension Jared's presence had created in her eased. Picking up silver tongs, she took ice cubes from the silver bucket on the bar and dropped one or two into each empty tumbler Vito set out. Twenty-five or so, slim and slightly shorter than average, he was a handsome young man and a very personable one too, as she discovered during the next few minutes. After she had taken Delia a martini and Angelina a margarita, she leaned against the bar, watching as he mixed her father's rum old-fashioned and answering the countless questions he asked her about her life in Vermont. He was easy to talk to, and with dark brown eyes that danced merrily and a persistent lock of hair that fell across his forehead, he seemed younger than he was and didn't make her feel as if she were balancing on the edge of a precipice as Jared did.

Her new-found tranquillity didn't last long, unfortunately. After giving her father his drink, she carried Jared a scotch and water. His lean fingers touched hers and lingered for a brief but electrifying instant before he took the glass from her hand. Her heart began to thud so wildly that she feared both he and Angelina must be able to hear it. Unable to look directly at him, she forced a little smile in response to his murmured thanks, then immediately returned to the bar.

"Now, what would you like to drink?" Vito asked, his eyes twinkling as he raked back the wayward lock of hair. Then he raised a hand to prevent her from answering. "Wait. Do not tell me. I will guess it." He stroked his chin thoughtfully. "It is difficult. A lovely young woman like you must drink some exotic concoction but I am not sure which one would suit you best. Perhaps a Brittany or a Rendezvous or a Polynesian Paradise?"

"Good heavens, no, I've never even heard of any of those drinks," Suzanne said, laughing softly at him. "I'm sorry to disappoint you but I'm really not an exotic person. So I think I'll just have a small glass of white wine."

"White wine?" Vito exclaimed, his voice rising. "Surely you want to have something stronger than that?"

"But, darling, she's just an infant," Delia remarked lazily from the sofa. "She's much too young to start drinking hard liquor. So don't you be a bad influence on her."

Though the words were spoken as if in jest, Suzanne

knew they were a deliberate attempt to put her in her place as well as embarrass her. So she merely smiled nonchalantly as the others laughed at her stepmother's "joke." After Vito handed her a glass of white wine as she had requested and got his own drink, they went to sit down on the sofa. With Jared and Angelina sharing the love seat and Delia poised prettily on the arm of the sofa, her arm draped across Jack's shoulders, the six of them had very effectively been divided into couples, as her stepmother had meant for them to be, Suzanne was certain. Yet it was a rather puzzling arrangement. If Delia really was involved with Jared, Suzanne couldn't imagine she was pleased that he was with a beautiful young woman like Angelina, unless, of course, Angelina was only a decoy. If she was being used to avert any possible suspicions about Jared and Delia's relationship, however, it appeared no one had bothered to tell her that. She seemed more than a little romantically interested in Jared and sat as close to him as possible, gazing at him with frank admiration.

For her father's sake, Suzanne hoped this meant Jared wasn't involved with Delia, but as far as she was concerned personally, she had to admit she wasn't thrilled with the possibility that he was Angelina's lover either. She was jealous, though she knew such an emotion was unjustifiable and unreasonable. Simply because he had kissed her once, she had no right to be jealous of Angelina. Yet it was impossible not to be as she watched the two of them sitting so closely together on the love seat.

Reminding herself repeatedly that it was no business of hers what Jared Caine did, Suzanne managed to somewhat enjoy the dinner that began fashionably at ten. With Vito beside her, giving her his complete attention, it didn't matter much that Delia, as usual, excluded her from the general conversation whenever possible. His lighthearted banter made it easier for Suzanne to ignore Angelina's persistent touching of Jared's hand or cheek or arm. Finally, after the main dish of lobster and the following lesser courses of cheese, fruit and dessert, the meal ended with coffee served in the salon. Sitting on the sofa with Vito again, Suzanne noticed that her father seemed to be tiring. Concerned about him, she wanted to suggest that he go upstairs to bed but Delia's continuous chatter never ceased long enough for Suzanne to speak.

At last it was Jared who made the suggestion that they call it a night. Moving forward on the love seat, he simply looked at Delia until she obviously realized he had something to say and fell mercifully silent for a minute. "It was a wonderful dinner. Thanks for inviting us, Delia, but I think Angelina and I should be going."

"Oh, but you can't go so soon!" Delia cried petulantly. "The evening's only just beginning. I insist you stay." With a foolish little giggle, she glanced coyly at Vito. "In fact, it's so early I was about to suggest you take Suzanne into Como to that nightclub you mentioned to me the other day. I'm sure both of you would enjoy that, wouldn't you? Suzanne really needs to get out into the social whirl more and you could introduce her to your friends. She needs to get acquainted with people nearer her own age."

"I would be delighted to take her," Vito agreed eagerly. Though he turned toward Suzanne, he apparently didn't detect the impatient gleam in her eyes because he smiled enthusiastically. "Would you like to go into Como? We could dance, perhaps, or. . . ."

"It's after twelve already," she said as kindly as she could. "I'm sure you have to work tomorrow so maybe we shouldn't be out late."

"Oh, but Vito is accustomed to late hours," Angelina spoke up, with a provocatively husky laugh as she gazed adoringly at Jared. "And I think it would be fun to go to this nightclub too, would it not, *caro?*"

Delia mumbled something beneath her breath and the displeased expression that aged her face made it quite obvious that she had not meant for Jared and Angelina to go with Vito and Suzanne. But before she could voice her thoughts, Jared himself ruined all her plans.

"If you'd like to go, Angel, it's fine with me." He looked at Delia. "I do think we should leave now. Jack's beginning to look tired."

Grimacing, Jack admitted very reluctantly, "I guess I am a little weary."

With a tight smile of sympathy for her husband, Delia nodded and patted his hand, apparently astute enough not to appear indifferent to his state of health. Still, her eyes glittered with some impatience as Jared stood, took Angelina's hand, and drew her up beside him.

"You wouldn't mind having us tag along with you and Suzanne, would you, Vito?" he asked, though his tone subtly indicated that he took acquiescence for granted. "That is, if Suzanne decides she wants to go at all."

With that statement, all eyes turned in Suzanne's direction and a faint blush tinted her cheeks. She hadn't really wanted to go with Vito in the first place and now that Jared and Angelina would be accompanying them, she was even less enthusiastic. She had no desire to spend the next few hours hearing him call the older girl "Angel" and making it sound like an intimate endearment. Yet, since everyone else wanted to go, she didn't want to become a spoilsport by refusing. At last, she nodded. "It sounds like fun," she lied. "I'd like to go."

"I do suggest we take both your car and mine," Vito said hastily. "We will have to, actually. There would not be room for us all in my Ferrari."

"We'll take my car then," Jared overruled him calmly. "There's plenty of room in it."

As Vito nodded rather reluctantly in agreement, Suzanne quickly rose to her feet, eager to escape Delia's indignant gaze. "Shall we go then—before it gets to be too late?"

"You'll need some sort of wrap," Jared declared, his dark eyes flicking over her. "It's a cool night."

"Not that cool, *caro,*" Angelina contradicted teasingly as she entwined her arm in his. "After all, my shoulders are bare but you did not tell me I needed a wrap when you came for me this evening."

"You're not recuperating from a bout of pneumonia," he replied succinctly. "Suzanne is, so she shouldn't risk catching a chill."

There was a certain stern note in his tone that Suzanne felt no inclination to argue with. Instead, she hastily excused herself to go up to her bedroom and get a cream-colored lightweight shawl, which she carried over her arm as she walked downstairs to the main hall where everyone was waiting. The guests were saying good night to her father and Delia and, as she hesitantly approached Vito, Jared intercepted her, reaching out to take the shawl. "It won't do you any good if you don't wear it," he said softly, proceeding to wrap the fine cashmere around her shoulders.

He was so close that Suzanne detected the spicy masculine fragrance of his aftershave and she watched his lean bronze hands with fascination as they brought the sides of the shawl together in front of her. His knuckles accidentally grazed the rounded curve of one breast and his touch was such a shock to her senses that she was scarcely able to prevent herself from gasping and stepping away from him. It was sheer willpower that enabled her to pretend that she hadn't noticed his touch at all—a willpower born out of her desire to appear at least somewhat sophisticated. The last thing in the world she wanted was for him to realize how physically attracted she was to him. And that meant she couldn't get flustered simply because he touched her inadvertently nor could she allow him to know she still felt self-conscious with him because he had kissed her. Undoubtedly, he had forgotten the incident and she wanted to act as blasé as he did about it. So as he released the shawl, she looked directly up at him and murmured her thanks for his help.

He made no response. Moving away from her, he cupped Angelina's elbow in his hand to escort her to the front door. Vito and Suzanne followed but before they stepped outside onto the dimly lighted portico, Delia called after them, "Don't keep Suzanne out too late now, Vito," she chanted. "Remember, she's just a baby compared to the girls you usually go out with."

"You do not look like a *bambina* to me," he teased softly, catching Suzanne's hand in his as they at last escaped outside.

Twenty minutes later, Jared parked the car along the lakefront in Como and the two couples crossed the street to enter what Vito had described as the most frequented nightclub in the town. Though they had already missed the performance of the featured singer, quite a number of patrons were still ensconced in booths with comfortable black leather seats or were seated along the mahogany bar, chatting quietly. Actually, it was more elegant than Suzanne had expected. Swinging Tiffany lamps with their stained glass shades provided a muted light that shimmered on the buffed wooden surface of the dancing area. In keeping with the late hour, a small band was playing soft romantic music.

"What would you like to drink?" Vito asked Suzanne as they settled themselves on the same side of the booth across the table from the older couple. "They have a special drink here that young ladies seem to prefer. Shall I order that for you?"

She shook her head. "I don't think I care for anything at all right now, thank you."

"You cannot come to a nightclub and not have a drink," he persisted, squeezing her hand, then smiling teasingly. "Surely you will at least have a glass of white wine, insipid as it is."

"Yes, all right, I'll have that," she agreed, trying not to notice that Angelina was presently whispering something into Jared's ear. Yet, during the next several minutes, she couldn't seem to relax, even after their drinks were brought and she had taken a few sips of the wine. Though Vito was a charming young man with a wonderful sense of humor, she was having a perfectly awful time and too often found herself glancing across the table at Jared. That was always a mistake which only served to make her feel worse still because Angelina was as close to him as she could get without sitting on his lap. For that reason, Suzanne was only too happy to accept Vito's invitation to dance after he had finished his drink.

On the dance floor, he held her more closely than she really wanted him to but she didn't resist. At least he kept time with the band as he hummed along in her ear. He didn't talk much. Instead, he seemed to lose himself in the music enabling her to do that too and when they stopped after about twenty minutes and went back to the booth, she was feeling more relaxed and contented. Neither feeling lasted long, however, because Jared and Angelina returned at the same moment. And before Suzanne could sit down and slide across the leather seat, he caught her hand.

"You promised me a dance, remember?" he murmured calmly, though it was an absolute untruth. And as she gazed up at him with wide surprised eyes and tried to tug free, his fingers merely tightened gently around hers. "Come with me."

Totally powerless to resist his softly persuasive command, Suzanne went. Though she sensed Vito's disapproval and could nearly feel Angelina's no longer limpid brown eyes boring holes in her back, she allowed Jared to lead her to the far edge of the dance floor. If she had thought that perhaps he was just being polite and would hold her at arm's distance, she was wrong. Slowly, he drew her to him, sliding both arms around her narrow waist so that she had no choice except to slip her own arms up across his broad shoulders. He was much taller than Vito. The top of Suzanne's head didn't quite reach his shoulder, which was both relieving and disturbing. At least their faces weren't on a level so she didn't have to look directly at him but, on the other hand, his very size was intimidating. As her softly rounded young body yielded to the firmer lineation of his, her heart felt as though it had leapt up into her throat and remained there for the next few minutes.

Though she had been kissed by him, she had never felt the strength of his arms enfolding her slenderness and the experience was far more intoxicating than any wine. He was an excellent dancer, easy to follow, and she felt as if she were floating on air. All that mattered at the moment was that the warmth that emanated from Jared's body enveloped her and her head nestled so comfortably into the hollow of his shoulder. Her eyes closed and she wished he could kiss her now and wondered how she would feel if he did.

He didn't talk much either. In fact, until she relaxed sufficiently to allow one hand to slip beneath the lapel of his navy blazer and her fingers spread open on the soft fabric of his white turtleneck, he said nothing at all. Then, he drew her even closer and lowered his head until his lips brushed against the scented thickness of her hair. "You smell delicious," was all he said. But it was enough.

Suzanne relaxed completely against his long lean body and considered the idea of never wearing any perfume other than the fragrance she had chosen to wear tonight. Yet, that was a foolish thought. Jared didn't *really* care what perfume she wore so it would be silly of her to try to please him. His provocative compliment had only been a fleeting response to her nearness and had conveyed no deeper hidden meaning. Neither had his kiss that day. Simply because one kiss had meant something to her, it didn't necessarily follow that it had meant anything to him and that was a fact she couldn't afford to forget. The realization was discouraging, however, and she sighed before she could prevent herself.

"You're tired," Jared misinterpreted the soft sound. Drawing away slightly, he surveyed her appealing face. "Maybe some fresh air will help." Without waiting for an answer from her, one muscular arm still around her waist, he led her out onto the flagstone piazza that faced the lake. Wrought iron lampposts with glass enclosed lights were set at regular intervals along the perimeter but their soft illumination wasn't needed tonight. A full cream-colored moon shone down, setting the placid surface of the lake ashimmer and bathing everything in a warming glow. A narrow flowerbed bordered the piazza, filling the air with the fragrance of cultivated jasmine and white ginger and roses. Bougainvillea vines spiraled upward on the lampposts, their blossoms swinging in a gentle breeze.

A man and woman embraced in the shadows and Suzanne glanced out of the corner of her eye at Jared, blushing as he suddenly looked down and caught her watching him. He gazed at the embracing couple for a moment, then back at Suzanne with an indulgent smile and a slight shrug. "Can you blame them? It's a night for lovers, don't you think?"

"That's the most beautiful moon I've ever seen," she answered evasively without really meaning to, her cheeks growing hotter as he laughed softly, almost knowingly. His hand around her waist warmed her skin through the fabric of her dress and she felt a sudden intense desire to slip her arm around him too but she didn't. Dismayed by her need to be closer to him, she tried to deny it by moving forward more swiftly than he did so that his arm dropped and she was free. After walking swiftly to the small stone fountain in the center of the piazza, she trailed her fingers through the pool in the upper basin along the edge where it cascaded down into the larger basin below. As Jared stepped up close behind her, her heart began to thud frantically. When his warm breath feathered over her hair, she trembled.

"Are you cold?" he murmured, his hands descending onto her shoulders, then slipping downward over the bare skin of her upper arms beneath the cap sleeves of her dress. "Why aren't you wearing your wrap?"

His fingertips slowly brushing over her sensitized skin were creating havoc with her senses. "I didn't need to wear it when we danced," she explained breathlessly. "It's . . . impossible to dance with a shawl falling from your shoulders."

"I see. Well, since you don't have it on, I'll put my coat around you."

"Oh, no. You don't need to do that."

"But if you're cold. . . ."

"But I'm not . . . not really."

"You must be," he whispered very close to her ear. "Why else would you be trembling the way you are?" As she stammered an incoherent answer, he covered her arms with his, crisscrossing them around her waist and drawing her back so close against him that her curved hips pressed against his hard thighs.

There was something so senuously evocative in his embrace that she could scarcely catch her breath and though she longed to relax against him, she simply couldn't allow herself to. He said nothing. He merely held her near, warming her with the heat of his lean body. Yet his silence so disconcerted her that she was compelled to break it by saying something, anything, so she babbled rather foolishly, "Angelina is a very beautiful woman."

For a few seconds he said nothing, then he agreed. "She is."

"You call her Angel," Suzanne said, her tone inadvertently accusing. "I mean. . . ."

"Almost everyone calls her Angel," Jared said softly. "At least, all her friends do."

"And are you her friend?"

"I've known her for a long time."

Afraid that was a deliberate evasion, Suzanne wondered what he was doing out here with her when Angelina, who was obviously much more than his friend, was waiting for him inside the nightclub. It did nothing for her ego to think he might simply feel protective of her because she was his business partner's daughter but it was a possibility she had to consider. After all, as Delia had so spitefully reminded her, he was a sophisticate and probably saw her as a child. At the thought, Suzanne sighed again, more dejectedly this time, and she was unable to look at Jared as he stepped around in front of her. Having lost the covering warmth of his arms, she shivered and as she did, his hands that still spanned her waist squeezed gently.

"What's wrong?" he murmured but she neither answered or looked up at him. "Suzanne?"

His oddly uneven tone made her lift her head. Though he was a dark silhouette with the moon behind him, the soft light illuminated her delicate features and glowed on her satiny smooth skin. Her eyes dilated and widened as he lifted one small hand and pressed a kiss against her palm. Fire danced over her skin and she was powerless to stop her fingers from curving against his cheek. With the tentative caress, his jaw hardened beneath her fingertips and he swiftly lowered his head. Too surprised to move or even gasp softly, she could only yield to his superior strength as one arm encircled her waist, lifted her up on tiptoe and crushed her against him. After guiding her hand to the strong column of his neck, he rained kisses over her cheeks and the smooth line of her jaw and the hollows beneath her ears as the cushioned ball of his thumb followed the shape of her eyebrows and the contours of her cheek-bones. When his firm lips covered hers, real passion stirred within her for the first time in her life and she was so overwhelmed by the intensity of this need to be closer to him that her fingers tangled in the thick dark hair on his nape as she clung to him.

"Open your mouth a little," he commanded huskily, then made her obey. His teeth closed tenderly on the curve of her lower lip, tugging until her mouth did open beneath his. The kiss deepened with irresistible swift-ness, became an intimate exploration. His lips were hard; she delighted in their strength as they pressed down into the softness of hers. When his hands moved over her back and around until his palms cupped the full firm sides of her breasts and the tip of his tongue tasted the sweetness of her mouth, she trembled violently, alive with sensations she had never truly believed existed until now. Yet, when she instinctively moved against him, he dragged his lips from hers with a soft groan and pulled her arms down from around his neck. Shaking his head, he put her away from him, his fingers pressing into the delicate hollows of her shoulders.

"I must be insane," he muttered self-derisively, his face shadowed and unreadable. "You're too young. . . ."

"I'm almost twenty-one," she protested defensively with a defiant uptilting of her chin. "I don't think that's so awfully young."

"It is when it's combined with innocence," he replied softly, his grip on her shoulders loosening slightly. He sighed. "Look, I'm just trying to apologize for what happened."

An apology for an experience she had found intensely pleasurable was the last thing Suzanne wanted. Totally humiliated, she chewed her lower lip and unhappiness darkened her eyes. She couldn't answer him. She had no idea what to say. All she knew was that he was sorry he had kissed her and that his regret caused a heavy aching in her chest. Now, she really did feel tired. Her shoulders dropped slightly beneath his hands and with an incomprehensible murmur, he pulled her close again and brushed her tousled hair back from her face.

"Don't look at me like that," he whispered. "I've said I'm sorry."

"I didn't ask you to," she replied tersely, holding herself stiffly in the circle of his arms. "In fact, I'd rather you didn't."

He lifted one dark brow. "Very well. I withdraw the apology."

"Good," she snapped, hurt concealing itself behind a veneer of defensive anger. "You obviously think I'm such a child that I'm surprised you didn't offer me a lollipop to soothe me instead of an apology."

"Don't be flippant," he growled, catching her chin between his thumb and forefinger, his dark eyes glittering. "Because I'm being very serious. I'm trying to warn you not to test your awakening sexuality on me. I'm not a schoolboy who'd be content with a couple of kisses. I'm a thirty-three-year-old man and I might expect you to finsih what you begin. Now, do you understand?"

She understood perfectly. There had been an unmistakable promise in his deep voice that sent a shiver of both fear and excitement trickling along her spine but as he felt her tremble, his hands dropped from her shoulders and he thrust them deep into the pockets of his trousers. "You see what I mean? You tremble whenever I touch you—so you obviously know you're playing with fire. So why don't we just go back into the club before I frighten you so much that your teeth begin to chatter."

Suzanne didn't have any choice except to go when he gripped her elbow roughly and impelled her toward the door that led into the dimly lighted room. As he marched her across the dance floor and over to the booth where Vito and Angelina sat, Suzanne squared her shoulders, determined not to show any indication that anything unusual had happened out on the piazza.

Unfortunately, Angelina's icy brown eyes swept over Suzanne, narrowing at the sight of her flushed cheeks, kiss-reddened mouth, and slightly tousled auburn hair; it was obvious she realized something had happened because her lips twisted derisively. The evening had been sufficiently disastrous already, so refusing to allow the older girl to make her feel any worse than she already did, Suzanne forced a very innocent smile. Then without waiting to observe the reaction to that smile, she turned to Vito as he rose to his feet.

"You are back. At last," he muttered, throwing Jared an impatient glance that vanished as he took Suzanne's hand. "Come. It is time for you to dance with me again."

"That's not a good idea, Vito," Jared announced. "It's late. We should go."

"Oh, *caro,* no!" Angelina protested, catching his hand in both hers, chastising him with her big brown eyes as if he had hurt her immeasurably with his suggestion. "I want to dance with you again. Please."

He shook his head. "Not tonight, Angel. It's nearly two o'clock and as I mentioned before, Suzanne's been ill. She's tired and, frankly, so am I."

Angelina had opened her mouth as if to argue further but apparently Jared's stern tone changed her mind. Clamping her lips together, she stood. "By all means, let us go then. I had forgotten that children need more sleep than adults do."

Ignoring the blatant insult, Suzanne smiled wanly at Vito and murmured her thanks as he draped the cashmere shawl around her shoulders. Unfortunately, Angelina's animosity only increased five minutes later, in the Jaguar. An uncomfortable silence followed Jared's announcement that he was taking her home first. She was far from pleased and with a toss of her thick raven hair, she glared back at Suzanne as if she blamed her completely for this latest disruption of her plans.

For that reason, it was a great relief when they arrived at Angelina's apartment building in the center of Como. As Jared saw her to her door, Vito draped his arm over Suzanne's shoulders, pulling her closer to his side. "I hope you will go out with me again very soon," he said softly. "Even though we have not been alone this evening, I have enjoyed it."

She hadn't but since that was hardly Vito's fault, she lied, "I enjoyed it too. It was . . . fun."

"Then you will say yes when I—" His words halted abruptly as Jared returned and slid in behind the steering wheel without a word.

The late hour and the nerve-racking scene with Jared on the piazza had begun to catch up with Suzanne, making her extremely tired. The swish of the tires on the smooth surface of the road nearly lulled her to sleep on the way home. When Jared stopped the car in front of the Collins' villa, her head had settled to rest on Vito's shoulder and he had to call her name to rouse her. Her eyes shot open, only to meet Jared's narrowed gaze as he stared back at her. She sat up straight, nervously tugging at the hem of her skirt. "I'm sorry, Vito," she muttered. "I didn't mean to use you as a pillow."

"It was my pleasure," he insisted charmingly. "Now, I will escort you to the door."

"Don't be long, Vito," Jared commanded brusquely as the younger man helped her from the car. "Remember, Suzanne needs her rest."

Her cheeks flamed and her green eyes sparkled with resentment as they darted over to meet his inscrutable gaze. Her indignation didn't appear to bother him in the least, however. He merely inclined his head, saying coolly, "Good night, Suzanne. I hope you sleep well."

Then you shouldn't have kissed me and then rejected me for responding, she thought resentfully. How could he possibly believe she might sleep well after what had happened between them? Unable to voice that question, however, she answered stiffly, "I'm sure I'll sleep like a baby . . . *if* I can locate my pacifier. I seem to have misplaced it."

"I hope you find it," he replied, only a slight upward tugging at the corners of his mouth betraying his amusement.

"He is as protective as an older brother," Vito commented a moment later as he and Suzanne crossed the portico. At the front door, he took her hands in his, then waited until the red taillights of the Jaguar had disappeared down the drive. "Alone at last," he whispered, pulling Suzanne into his arms.

His kiss was uninspiring and she couldn't respond. All she could think about was the tumultuous emotions Jared's hard yet gentle lips had evoked in her. Vito's kiss couldn't compete though she wished desperately that it could. Her life certainly would be simpler if she were attracted to him rather than to a complex, confusing man like Jared Caine.

Chapter Five

Wednesday afternoon, Jack Collins summoned Suzanne to his study. Against the advice of his doctor, he had now begun to work at home several hours a day, insisting that he would recover his strength much faster if he kept busy. And Suzanne was beginning to agree with him. As she entered the study, she immediately noticed that his coloring was better and there was a definite air of vitality about him as he shuffled through a stack of papers on his desk.

He glanced up and motioned her into the chair that faced him. After finding the document he wanted and perusing it for a minute or so, he put it aside, then leaned back in his swivel chair. "Italy seems to agree with you," he said. "You're less pale than you were."

"I was thinking the same thing about you," she admitted. "Except that it's work that seems to agree with you. As long as you don't overdo, of course."

"Don't worry. I know how to pace myself. Now, enough of that boring subject. I didn't call you in here to talk about my health. I want to talk about you." His expression solemn, he leaned forward again, resting his arms on the desk top. "Delia tells me you act as if you'd like to leave soon. Why? Aren't you happy here?"

"I can't imagine what I've done to give Delia that impression," Suzanne said, wondering what kind of game her stepmother was trying to play now. "I really hadn't given much thought to going back to Vermont yet. I thought I'd stay here a few more weeks unless . . . you'd rather I didn't?"

"What kind of question is that?" her father exclaimed irritably. "Why on earth would I want you to leave?"

Suzanne spread her hands in a helpless gesture. "I don't know. I just wondered . . . I mean, you and Delia are accustomed to being alone and with me around. . . ."

"I like having you around! You're my daughter and you're welcome here."

"Then I'll stay awhile," Suzanne murmured and started to stand. "Now that that's settled, I'll run along and let you get back to your paper work."

"Wait. There's something else I want to discuss with you." Tapping the end of a pencil on the desk top, he eyed her speculatively. "Delia also mentioned that although you don't know many people here, you turned Vito down the past two evenings when he called to ask you out. She was surprised you didn't jump at the chance to go out with such an eligible young man, who's apparently quite taken with you. Is there some reason why you turned him down? Don't you like him?"

"Sure I do; he's very nice," Suzanne replied honestly. "But . . . well, he seems interested in a romantic relationship and I'm not."

"And you don't want to encourage him by going out with him?" When she agreed, Jack nodded. "Well, I can understand that but Delia likes Vito. She'd like to see you go out with him. She doesn't want you to be lonely while you're here."

"I like to form my own relationships," Suzanne said flatly, not the least bit convinced that her stepmother felt any genuine concern for her. "Besides, I'm not really lonely. I've always been able to entertain myself. I love to go for walks here; the countryside is so beautiful. Or I can read."

"And what about that sketch pad you have with you? I've seen you doodling in it. Are you making sketches for a painting you want to do?"

"Nothing so ambitious," Suzanne replied wryly. "I'd planned to batik some fabric for drapes for our apartment. I've been trying to come up with a design I like. Finally, I have, but I'm afraid it may be too complicated."

"Could I take a look at it?" Jack asked, surprising her with his interest. "After all, I know a little about fabric design now that we're in the silk business."

After turning to the right page, Suzanne handed the sketchbook to her father, then leaned across his desk as he looked at it. "See what I mean," she said, following with one fingertip a ribbon of royal blue she had colored onto a light tan background. "I think I've intertwined the swirls too intricately. I like it that way but it's too complex for a batik design. It would take an eternity to apply the wax on fabric so only the swirls were dyed blue."

Jack nodded. "It certainly would. But this is a lovely design, perfect for silk scarves. And we're always looking for new ones." He gave her a smile reminiscent of the ones he had given her before her mother had died. "How would you like me to hand this over to the design department? Wouldn't it be fun to know that some of the chic women of Europe were wearing your creation?"

Suzanne smiled enthusiastically. "I think I'd like that very much."

"Well, then, I'll give it to Jared the next time I see him."

"Maybe we should just forget the whole thing," she murmured, her enthusiasm dying a quick death. "I'm sure Mr. Caine wouldn't want to bother with my design."

"Nonsense. I told you we're always looking for new designs and sometimes they're hard to come up with. Jared will be happy to get this one. It's very original. He might even want to pay you for it."

"But he might not agree that it's good," she persisted, reluctant to allow Jared to judge anything she had created. "I don't think you should give it to him."

With a shrug, Jack pushed the design to the side of his desk, his expression suddenly brooding. "You not only look like your mother, you act like her too. She could be unbelievably stubborn at times."

"I'm not trying to be stubborn. I just don't want Mr. Caine to feel like I asked you to force him to accept my design," Suzanne explained, gesturing uncertainly. "You understand?"

"No problem. Let's just forget it," her father replied curtly, becoming remote again.

As he turned in his swivel chair and began rifling through a desk drawer, Suzanne bit down hard on her lower lip. He was never again going to be the warm and loving father she had once known and the sooner she accepted that, the better off she'd be. Certain he had nothing further to say to her today, she started walking quietly toward the door but stopped immediately when he asked her to wait.

"Will you do me a favor, if you're not going to be busy for the next half hour or so? Delia meant to drop this wage scale proposal off at Jared's villa on her way to go shopping but she left and forgot to take it. Would you mind driving over there with it?"

"I don't know where Jared lives," Suzanne reminded

him quickly. "Couldn't you just call and ask him to come pick up the proposal?"

"He's not home right now but I want this proposal there waiting for him when he does arrive. He needs to look it over."

Since there was no chance of her having to see Jared, Suzanne saw no reason why she shouldn't go. After all, she had been wanting to see his villa. She nodded. "I'll take it over then, if it's that important, and if you'll tell me how to get there."

"Just follow the road up around the first curve, and take the first driveway to the right."

"I didn't realize Jared lived so near here."

"So you see, this errand won't take you long. Here's the proposal. Just ask Jared's housekeeper to put it on his desk."

Taking the manila envelope her father held out, she smiled. "Since the villa's so close, I don't need to drive. I'll just walk."

"Well, it's not all that close. And I don't want you walking nearly a half mile up that steep winding road. Some people drive like maniacs on it." Jack shook his head. "No, take the BMW. Ask Pietro for the keys."

Five minutes later, by the back door, Suzanne found the handyman tending his garden. But when she requested the car keys, he grimaced and spread his hand expressively. "*Scusa, signorina,* but the *meccanico* from Como came to take the car for a . . . how you say it? A tone-up?"

"Tune-up," she corrected automatically, tapping one finger against her lips. "Oh, well, I guess I will walk to Mr. Caine's villa after all, since there's no car to drive."

"The *signorina* can ride a motorbike, perhaps?" Pietro inquired hopefully. "My grandson, he will not mind if you borrow his for a short time."

The idea appealed to her. Although it had been quite some time since she had ridden a motorbike, she was sure she could handle one. After nodding her agreement, she followed Pietro to the side drive where a gleaming red Morini cycle stood, propped up by its metal kickstand. With a mischievous grin, she hopped on and started the engine. Then she was on her way, weaving slightly along the driveway with her first jerky accelerations. By the time she turned out onto the road, however, she was going along fairly steadily, without weaving from side to side at all.

Her hair flowed out behind her in the wind that cooled her shapely bare legs. Proud of her expertise on the bike, she accelerated immediately after veering off onto the first asphalt drive to the right after passing the curve. Umbrella pines lined the winding driveway, their green floretlike tops swaying in the breeze. Driving beneath a stone arch festooned by bougainvillea vines laden with scarlet blooms, she bypassed the entrance to a flagstone courtyard and followed the drive as it circled in front of the villa. As she slowed down, unfortunately, Jared stepped out from the shadowed portico and the sight of him so unnerved her she inadvertently jerked the handlebars sharply to the right. Skidding into the white pebbled border edging the drive, she lost her balance and the bike went on without her for a brief distance when she was ignominiously tossed to the ground. Impact knocked the breath from her body and although she was aware of a stinging sensation along the side of her right leg, the physical pain of that minor injury really didn't matter at the moment. She was too busy berating herself for looking like a clumsy oaf in front of Jared.

After managing to catch her breath again, she struggled to sit up on the grass where she had landed. Hot color suffused her cheeks as Jared reached her, dropping down onto his knees by her side.

"Are you all right?" he muttered urgently, his lean hands amazingly gentle as he lightly gripped her upper arms. "Have you hurt yourself?"

"Only my dignity," she replied, her voice embarrassingly squeaky. "But would you check the bike? It belongs to Pietro's grandson. He'll probably murder me if I scratched the paint."

"To hell with the bike!" Jared said curtly, examining her from head to toe. A deep frown furrowed his brow; his eyes narrowed as he noticed the scraped side of her right leg. His hand came down, his fingertips feathering over the tender skin and when she took a sharp breath, his jaw hardened. "Does it hurt that much?"

"It only hurts a little," she murmured, trying to conceal the fact that his touch had been more disturbing than painful. "It's not even bleeding; it just stings a bit. I'm just lucky only my leg landed in the pebbles."

"You might have broken it . . . or your neck," he scolded, an impatient gleam flaring in the depths of his dark eyes. "Why the devil are you riding that ridiculous bike anyway?"

"Dad asked me to bring some proposal over here so you'd have it to look over when you came home this evening," she explained, her words coming out in a rush. "The BMW's in the shop for a tune-up and since Delia took the Volante into Como to go shopping, I . . . well, when Pietro offered me his grandson's bike, I thought it might be fun to ride it over." She smiled wanly. "Dad told me you wouldn't be here."

"So you wouldn't have minded taking this spill if I hadn't been here to see it?" he questioned sharply. "Is that what you mean?"

"I probably wouldn't have run into the gravel if you

hadn't stepped out of the shadows so unexpectedly and scared me half to death," she answered, her tone equally sharp. "Until I saw you, I was handling the bike very expertly."

A muscle in his jaw ticked with fascinating regularity. "Are you blaming me for this little mishap?"

"You weren't supposed to be here," she repeated, picking herself up, brushing off, and wrinkling her nose at the grass stain on her crisp khaki shorts. "But no, I'm not blaming you; it isn't your fault I haven't ridden a motorbike in a long time." Tugging at the hem of her green tee shirt, she glanced up at him and groaned inwardly. It simply wasn't fair for her to look so messy right now when he was as irresistibly attractive as ever in close fitting navy trousers and a white rugby-styled shirt. As usual, there was an aura of virility surrounding him that upset her equilibrium and she took a step backward. Although she hadn't seen him since Sunday night when they had gone to the nightclub with Angelina and Vito, she hadn't forgotten for a minute that he thought of her as a child. And she was still very disappointed that he did because she had never felt less like a child than she did whenever he was near. Yet if he didn't want to see her as a woman, there was nothing she could do to change his mind, she reminded herself bleakly. Smoothing her windswept hair, she avoided his probing gaze by staring past him at the fallen motorbike.

"Well, I don't want to take up any more of your time," she announced finally, stepping by him. "I'll give you the proposal, then be on my way."

As she walked to the motorbike, Jared followed and took the manila envelope out of her hand after she had removed it from the leather bag attached to the back of the seat. Then he caught her hand, holding her fast. "Thanks for bringing this but don't expect me to let you leave until we've attended to your leg. You're not going anywhere."

"I'm going home," she argued, trying to snatch her hand free. When his grip only tightened, she sighed. "Look, you needn't worry about my leg. It just needs to be washed off."

"Antiseptic is in order too, I think," he said implacably, impelling her toward the portico with its graceful fluted columns.

For the first time, Suzanne really noticed the villa. It was exquisite, a sunwashed white jewel in the setting of lush greenery. Lombardy pines formed a semicircle behind the three-story structure, which overlooked the crystalline blue lake. Terraced gardens stepped up the rolling hill beyond the flagstone courtyard and the fragrance of pittosporum hedges and the fresh pinelike scent of rosemary perfumed the air. Despite the fact that Suzanne longed to see inside the villa, however, she dragged her feet. "I'd rather go home," she murmured weakly, gazing up at Jared, her green eyes wide. "Really."

He shook his head, his stern expression clearly indicating he would tolerate no nonsense. "I intend to see that leg gets proper attention so don't act like a baby. The antiseptic won't sting all that much."

"You enjoy baiting me, don't you?" she mumbled indignantly but allowed him to lead her to the front door. He opened it and as they stepped into the vast main gallery, she exclaimed with delight. Their footfalls rang on muted amber and cream tiles and as Jared guided her toward closed double doors, she gazed in awe at the vaulted ceiling above and at the frescoed walls which depicted fading but still lovely pastoral scenes.

"Oh, Jared, it's beautiful," she whispered when he opened the carved wooden doors and she preceded him into the salon. A colorful Rabat rug adorned the center of the white, veined marble floor and arranged around the rug, antique mahogany chairs and sofas were upholstered in delicately designed red and black tapestry that echoed the predominant colors in the carpet. A round table bearing a crystal vase filled with flaming scarlet poppies stood before the tall narrow window overlooking the portico. At the opposite end of the room, in front of the French windows that opened onto the piazza, there was another sofa and two chairs arranged around a low carved table. At intervals along the frescoed walls were dark side tables, each topped with a vase of the scarlet poppies and in a glass-enclosed case, there was a menagerie of small jade and ivory animals.

Fascinated by everything she saw, Suzanne was speechless and automatically sank down on one of the central sofas, to which Jared led her.

"I'll go get a basin of water and the antiseptic," he informed her and after she nodded absently, he left the salon.

Watching as he strode away, Suzanne hastily ran her fingers through her hair, trying to tidy it before he returned. She wished he had let her go home since she obviously irritated him immensely. With a sigh of dismay, she leaned down to look at her leg and when she gingerly touched it, she was amazed that such a superficial injury could sting so much. Then she heard footsteps on the marble tiled floor in the main gallery and sat up straight again, her heartbeat accelerating despite all her efforts to control its pace.

Jared strode across the salon and, kneeling before her on the carpet, he gently washed her scraped skin with sterile cotton soaked in warm water. And, without giving her any warning whatsoever, he applied a clear antiseptic liquid. Though it burned like the very devil, Suzanne made no sound. She merely ground her teeth together, unwilling to show any reaction. As Jared looked up at her, she forced a tight little smile, which obviously didn't fool him.

"Sorry," he murmured, drying his hands on the small towel he had brought. "But you know it's important to clean scrapes."

"Of course. Now, it'll heal faster, I hope," she said wryly. "Even so, for the next few days, I'm going to look like I've been in a cat fight."

As Jared put the basin of water aside and rose to his feet, his gaze drifted along the slender length of her legs. He shook his head, saying quietly, "I don't agree. One scrape can't make such shapely legs less lovely."

Gulping, Suzanne stood also. "Well, I'd better be going. You're busy, I'm sure, so I'll just leave."

As she started to step past him, he moved to block her way. "Why go now? Stay and I'll show you the villa. Then you can decide if Delia's right and it needs redecorating." A hint of a smile touched his firmly shaped lips. "All right? Wouldn't you like to look around?"

"Oh, yes, I'd love to," she exclaimed softly, enthusiasm lighting her face. "But only if you're sure you have the time to give me a tour."

"If I didn't have time, I wouldn't have offered," he replied logically, catching her hand in his. "Come on. We'll begin in the library."

Suzanne was fascinated by the vast book-lined room located across the main gallery from the salon. Despite its spaciousness, it was cozy and the worn brown leather sofa and winged-back chairs were inviting. "What a perfect place to spend a rainy day," she commented almost wistfully as they walked out into the gallery again, past the foot of the wide marble stair-case. "It must be very warm and snug in there when it's damp and chilly outside."

"Yes, and I can imagine you curled up like a kitten in one of the chairs, your nose buried in a book," Jared answered wryly. "Or else you'd be lost in a daydream. That's why you like rainy days, isn't it? Because you can give free rein to your imagination?"

"How did you know that? Most people think I'm nuts to enjoy an occasional day of rain. Don't you think that too?"

"No, I don't think that," he replied, amusement dancing in his eyes as he looked down at her. "I wouldn't call you nuts exactly. Perhaps a little eccen-tric, but that can be a very charming attribute." With a smile and an exaggerated sweeping gesture of one hand, he threw open the door to a smaller salon and indicated by inclining his head that she should precede him. "If you liked the library, I think you'll like this."

"Oh, I do," she agreed, thinking it was the most appealing room she had ever seen. The decor wasn't at all fancy, the furniture was done in dark blue and beige tapestry and there was an expensive Oriental rug, predominantly blue, covering most of the tiled floor. It was the lack of frills that gave the room an elegant simplicity. There was a bronze horse rearing up on a thick base, its texture rough, though the lines of its sinewy muscles were flowing and incredibly lifelike. That and a lovely antique bowl, enameled in blue and beige with a thin veining of red, were the only objects on a long low table that sat against the far wall. Heavy cut glass decanters and glasses graced the top of a mahogany liquor cabinet sitting against the frescoed side wall. Beside the chair that matched the sofa was a round table bearing a brass lamp and an opened book placed face down as if someone had just gone away and left it there.

"I spend most of my leisure time in here," Jared said unnecessarily.

"I was sure you must," Suzanne responded with a knowing smile. "This room looks like you. It's . . . masculine." As his dark eyebrows lifted and he held her gaze, she looked away self-consciously and hastened to the door.

After getting a glimpse of a large well-lighted kitchen with a wooden chopping block in the center of the floor and all the modern conveniences unobtrusively incorporated into the old world decor, Suzanne walked with Jared back into the main gallery. As he paused at the foot of the winding marble stairs, she glanced upward hopefully. "Could I see up there too?" she asked somewhat hesitantly. "I mean, if you have time to show it to me."

He only smiled indulgently, then took her hand again as they walked up the wide steps and entered the upstairs gallery. During the next twenty minutes, Suzanne admired the large elegant bedrooms, all with adjoining tiled baths but really it was Jared's own room she was eager to see. He took her there last and when he opened the carved double doors, she wasn't disappointed. This was so obviously a man's room too, done in earth colors: russet, tan and brown. The furniture was dark and heavy yet not oppressively so because of its simple lines. A carved arched door opened into the adjoining bathroom but there was only a bit of carving on the head and footboards of the high wide bed, which sat on a plush brown area rug and was covered by a russet and tan tapestry spread. It was the frescoed wall behind the headboard that captured Suzanne's attention and she walked across the room to take a closer look. Though the colors were fading, the fresco clearly depicted the lake with the hills rising up on the opposite shore.

"Why, that's the view you have from the front of the villa, isn't it?" she exclaimed softly. "Oh, it's wonderful. How did the artist ever capture it in such detail before the plaster dried?"

"It required skill as well as artistic talent," Jared said, then grimaced regretfully. "Unfortunately, it's an artform rarely practiced these days. This fresco was done approximately three centuries ago."

"And after all this time, it's still beautiful," she whispered. Then without really thinking, she compulsively laid her hand on his forearm and her tone took on an urgency, "Don't let Delia change any of this, Jared, please. This is the way a villa should look. Don't let her redecorate it."

"I never intended to," he said softly, his own free hand coming up to cover the smaller one touching his arm. "Did you really think I'd let her turn my home into a showcase of modern furnishings?"

With the brushing motion of his fingers on her skin, her breathing became shallower, faster. The tip of her tongue appeared to moisten suddenly dry lips and when he took a step closer, a nearly overpowering awareness of the wide bed beside them gripped her. She turned aside, sliding her hand out from beneath his as she stepped through the open French doors onto the balcony. A wrought iron railing supported climbing stems laden with both crimson and ivory rosebuds and their fragrance filled the air even though the blooms were not yet open. Suzanne took a deep breath as Jared stepped close behind her. Trying to relax, she looked down at the terraced gardens, watching as a lanky yellow dog ambled along the paths, sniffing, seeking whatever it is that dogs habitually seek.

"The gardens are beautiful," she said nervously, glancing over her shoulder up at him. "Could . . . do you have time to let me see them?"

"You're obsessed by time," he teased, then nodded. "But yes, I think a walk in the gardens might be a very good idea."

The gardens were enclosed by fragrant pittosporum hedges, the dark green foliage scattered with small waxy white flowers. A few minutes later, when Jared and Suzanne walked through the arched entrance, she inhaled appreciatively and tried to identify some of the innumerable blooms in a myriad of colors that lifted their velvety petals up to catch the life-sustaining rays of the sun. Purple fuchsia blossoms nodding in the breeze bordered the path that led to an arbor surrounded by white camellia shrubs. A white wooden-slatted bench encircled the deeply grooved trunk of an ancient juniper. While Suzanne sat down, Jared picked a perfect camellia blossom and handed it to her. After she accepted it with a bemused smile, he sat down on the bench beside her, stretching his long legs out in front of him as he leaned back against the rough trunk.

"How's it going between Jack and you," he asked abruptly. "I know the two of you aren't as close as you should be. But I had hoped this visit would change that."

"You're very perceptive—Dad and I aren't very close anymore," she said, twirling the flower stem between her fingers. "I'm beginning to doubt we'll ever be close again."

"Is that why you want to go back to Vermont? Delia said—"

"I know what Delia said. She also told Dad I was thinking of leaving," Suzanne interrupted with an impatient toss of her hand. "Frankly, I don't know where she got that idea. I certainly haven't said anything to her about wanting to go back to Vermont. Maybe it's just wishful thinking on her part; I'm sure she'd be delighted if I did leave. Some stepmothers don't want their stepchildren around."

"And some of them do," Jared reminded her softly. "Are you sure you're not judging Delia unfairly?"

"Why do you always leap to her defense?" Suzanne retorted suspiciously. "Do you think she's such a warm person that she *must* shower me with affection? You always assume it's my fault that I'm not close to her. Why? Do you see her as such a lovable person?"

"My stepmother is," he answered surprisingly. "She married my father when I was eight and she's always treated me as if I were her own son."

"You're lucky then," Suzanne muttered. "Some of us aren't so fortunate."

"Maybe you haven't given Delia a fair chance."

His defense of Delia made Suzanne feel betrayed somehow and she wanted the entire conversation to cease. "I don't want to talk about her anymore." she said. "Okay?"

"Fine. Then tell me why you can't be close to Jack anymore."

"Because he won't let me!" Suzanne exclaimed softly, the unhappiness she had suppressed for too long finally erupting. Tears filled her eyes. "He won't let me be close to him. Since Mother died, he's been so aloof. I've needed to share my memories of her with him but until I came for this visit, he never once mentioned her to me. And the two times he's mentioned her this summer were only to say that I look very much the way she did." She bent her head and a soft sob caught in her throat as she added, "Don't you think I'd like to be close to him? He won't let me. I just don't mean a lot to him anymore."

"That's not true," Jared argued gently, lifting her

chin with one forefinger. "Jack often talks about how proud he is of you. Maybe he simply can't allow himself to be very close. If you do look like your mother did, you might arouse memories that he finds very painful because he lost her."

A fat crystalline teardrop rolled down Suzanne's cheek. "I never thought of that," she murmured thickly. "But I know he did love her very much so I guess he could be cool to me because I remind him too much of her."

"I imagine that's it exactly," Jared said comfortingly.

As another teardrop followed the path of the first, Suzanne moved gratefully into the haven of Jared's arms as he drew her to him. Her head rested against his hard chest and she felt more secure than she had in a very long time. She had thought she had lost her father's love forever, but Jared's theory eased a hurt she had endured for many years. Wrapping her arms around his waist, she snuggled closer and luxuriated in the pleasure of simply being held for several minutes.

Unreasonably, it was the lilting song of a skylark as it soared upward in its flight above them that changed everything. Suzanne felt Jared's body tense against her own and before she could react, he had wound her thick hair around one hand, pulled her head back slightly, and sought her mouth. There was little initial gentleness in his kiss this time. Ever hardening lips plundered the sweet softness of hers. As the tip of his tongue teased first one corner then the other of her mouth, she moaned softly as her arms went up to encircle his neck. His kiss deepened urgently when her body became pliant beneath his questing hands. Suzanne trembled with delight as he kissed her closed eyelids, the hollows of her cheeks, then her lips again with ravishing passion. An unfamiliar emptiness awakened in her and clamored to be filled as his hands cupped the fullness of her breasts, burning her skin through the thin knit fabric of her shirt and the sheer lace of her bra. Liquid fire surged through her veins and she was powerless to prevent her own hands from covering his to press them harder against her throbbing flesh.

"Suzanne!" he groaned, as his fingers tightened momentarily. "Don't make me want you any more than I already do."

"Jared," she whispered, brushing her lips over the strong tendons of his neck. "Please kiss me again."

"Suzanne," he whispered back hoarsely before his lips took hers again, then dragged his mouth from hers with obvious reluctance. His dark eyes glimmered with hot desire. "You are too young."

"No," she contradicted breathlessly. "I'm not a child."

"Why do you look like one then?" he asked tautly, stilling the fingers that caressed his lean cheek.

"I can't help how I look. I *am* almost twenty-one, not fourteen or fifteen." Held in his arms, she smiled up at him with drowsy green eyes. "And if you're seducing me, I think I like it."

"Enough to allow it to be a totally successful seduction?" he countered roughly, his gaze narrowing. "This is my housekeeper's day off so we have the villa to ourselves. Are you willing to go back up to my bedroom with me? Right now?"

"No!" she gasped, her cheeks paling as she struggled to sit up straight. "You . . . I couldn't do that!"

"No, I thought not," he replied coolly, rising to his feet. Thrusting his hands in his pocket, he shook his head. "Go home, Suzanne. I don't play games with children."

She lost her temper. Once again she had put herself in a position where he could reject her and she was as furious with herself as she was with him. She jumped up. "Well, I don't play games at all, Mr. Caine, so I'd be happy to go home. And stop calling me a child. I don't like it."

As she rushed away, she heard him laughing softly. She squeezed her hands into fists as she marched on, wishing she had never even heard of him, much less met him. He was an impossible man and she would be happy if she never spoke to him again.

Chapter Six

Suzanne's birthday began pleasantly. Early morning sunlight filled her room with a lemon yellow glow and the warming rays released the sweet fragrance of the white jasmine that grew in a long narrow box on her balcony. A gentle breezed promised to keep the day from becoming excessively hot and as Suzanne slipped into a denim sundress, she decided it would be a nice morning to go for a long walk. Humming softly, she caught her hair back, securing the entire silken swathe in a plain gold barrette on her nape. After stepping into leather sandals, she left her room and ran lightly down the stairs.

No one was in the dining room when she arrived, but there was the typical overabundance of food in covered warming dishes on the sideboard. Luckily, she was hungrier than usual this morning and served herself shirred eggs in addition to the freshly baked croissant and cup of coffee she always had. Ten minutes later, as she was finishing her breakfast, her father came into the dining room and when she looked up, she received a very mysterious smile from him.

She smiled back but her eyes widened incredulously when he stopped by her chair and brought two gilt-wrapped packages from behind his back. "You remembered?" she said disbelievingly. "I didn't think you would."

He grimaced sheepishly. "Just because I'm always at least two weeks late remembering your birthday, you shouldn't have assumed I would forget it again this year."

Her green eyes danced with a mischievous light at his teasing tone. "Oh, of course I shouldn't have," she teased back. "But I learned long ago that you have a notoriously bad memory for dates so I never imagined you would turn over a new leaf this year."

"I was so ashamed of myself last year when I was three weeks late sending you a present that I circled today's date on every calendar I own so I couldn't possibly forget this year." After putting the packages on the table beside Suzanne's plate, her father went to the sideboard to pour a cup of black coffee. "So, how does it feel to be twenty-one years old?"

"The same as it did to be twenty," she answered honestly, lightly touching the white ribbons and bows that adorned the gold-wrapped gifts. Smiling at her father as he sat down across the table from her, she lifted her shoulders in a slight shrug. "Really, I don't suddenly feel wiser just because I'm a year older today."

He smiled back. "Well, aren't you going to open your presents?"

Nodding, she slowly slipped the ribbon and bow off and removed the gilt paper, careful not to tear it though she knew it would never be used again. Inside she found a rectangular jeweler's box and, on opening it, found an exquisitely delicate gold Victoria chain. "Oh, Dad, it's beautiful. I love it," she said sincerely, putting the necklace on and securing the clasp at her nape. With one fingertip she followed the chain as it curved into the hollow at the base of her throat, then quickly got up to look into the mirror above the sideboard. The gold glimmered warmly next to her lightly tanned skin.

At Jack's prompting, she sat down again to open the second gift, which was a bracelet to match the necklace. After securing it, she extended her arm, admiring the way the smooth sides of the links reflected the light. She smiled at her father. "They're beautiful, Dad. Thank you."

"Isn't that bracelet too big?" he asked, frowning slightly. "It won't slip off, will it?"

"Oh, no, it's fine," she assured him with a smile. "And so is the necklace. You couldn't have chosen anything I would have liked more. Thank you again."

As she got up, went around the table, and gave him a kiss, he squeezed her hand, then smiled a bit sheepishly. "Actually, I can't take the credit for choosing this particular style of necklace and bracelet. Since the doctor won't allow me to go to town, I had to ask someone to do the shopping for me."

"Delia picked these out?" Suzanne asked, surprised that her stepmother hadn't chosen something much more flamboyant than these simple chains.

"No, Delia planned to shop for me but she's been very busy lately so she never got around to it," Jack explained. "So, when I realized time was running out, I asked Jared to choose a matching bracelet and necklace in a style he thought you'd like. He said these suited you perfectly. I'm glad to see he was right."

"It was nice of him to take the time to do it. I must remember to thank him," Suzanne murmured, trying to conceal the fact that it made her inordinately happy that Jared thought these simple yet elegantly feminine chains suited her. It was silly of her to feel that way. His choice of a gift only meant that he had good taste in jewelry, not that he had taken any real personal interest in choosing something for her.

"Well, I've dawdled over breakfast long enough,"

Jack said, interrupting his daughter's reverie. Pushing back his chair, he stood, looking down at her. "What are your plans for the morning?"

"I thought I'd take a walk."

"You'll be back in time for lunch though, won't you? Delia's still sleeping now but she bought a gift for you yesterday. She asked me to tell you to be sure you're here for lunch today so she can give it to you."

"All right, I'll be here," Suzanne agreed, then a wry smile curved her lips as her father left the dining room. Life certainly was full of surprises sometimes. She had never expected Delia to even remember her birthday, much less to go to the trouble of buying her a gift.

Suzanne enjoyed her walk through the woods above the villa, but at twelve o'clock she left the shade of the trees and started for home. She walked diagonally down the sloping meadow that adjoined her father's property, stopping occasionally to admire the carpeting of blue wildflowers that swayed in the breeze. Streaks of gray rock slashed through the green grass, some of them rising upward high enough to become stark outcroppings, adding to the wild unspoiled beauty of the countryside. Although the scenery was lovely and the breeze was cooling, Suzanne didn't linger long in the meadow. The midday sun beating down on her bare head made her eager to take a refreshing shower before lunch.

As soon as she reached the villa, she ran lightly up the stairs, intending to go straight to her room. Unfortunately, just as she was passing the door to Delia's suite, Lucia opened the door and started out, bearing a tray laden with a small silver coffeepot and a delicate china saucer and cup, the remains of what the everdieting Delia laughingly called her "breakfast." Suzanne glanced into the room at the same moment her stepmother turned from her vanity mirror and glanced out into the hall.

As Delia beckoned her inside imperiously, Suzanne went into the room, although with a certain amount of reluctance. And when she caught the pained expression that flitted across her stepmother's perfectly made-up face, she steeled herself for the derogatory statement she felt certain was about to follow.

Delia didn't surprise her. Shaking her head disapprovingly, she gave a rather impatient sigh. "Surely you don't plan to wear that denim thing down to lunch?" she asked snobbishly. "You look like a peasant. I would think you could put on something more stylish, today at least. After all, it is your birthday."

Hands clasped behind her back, Suzanne looked down impassively at the older woman. "I was just on my way to my room to shower and change," she said coolly. "So if you'll excuse me. . . ."

"You've been out for a walk, I suppose," Delia drawled, turning back to the mirror. After arranging a short tendril of hair at her temple, she sprayed it with hair lacquer to keep it in place. "I can always tell when you've been out on one of your hikes. You come back with your cheeks as flushed as the girls who pick the grapes in the vineyards."

"I save a lot of money on blusher by going on walks instead," Suzanne replied laconically, unable to resist a rather pointed glance at Delia's well-stocked vanity. "Now, I'd better run have my shower or I'll be late for lunch."

"I have a present for you," her stepmother informed her tautly. "But I think I'll just wait until after lunch to give it to you. And we have a guest, so come down on time."

"I'll do my best," Suzanne said, beating a hasty path

out the door. As she continued along the gallery to her own room, she smiled rather wickedly to herself. Perhaps Delia's present would turn out to be a gift certificate for a free chemical peel that would eliminate all those gauche little freckles from her face.

Twenty-five minutes later, Suzanne was ready for lunch. She allowed her hair to swing unconfined down around her shoulders and the golden highlights of the auburn tresses shimmered whenever she moved her head. The soft silken strands caressed bare skin exposed above the tucked bodice of her cream-colored gauze sundress and as she examined her reflection in the cheval glass, she wondered whether this attire would please Delia. Probably not, but Suzanne really didn't care. She had no intention of letting her stepmother rule her life.

Delia had other ideas, however, as Suzanne discovered the moment she walked downstairs and into the salon. The lunch guest turned out to be Vito Gallio, who rose up from the white velvet sofa when he saw her and rushed across the room with an exuberant smile. "Happy birthday, Suzanne," he said softly, then gave her a light kiss on the lips. Slipping his arm around her waist, a too possessive gesture, he led her back toward the sofa. "It pleases me a great deal that you wanted me to share this special occasion. Thank you for asking Delia to invite me today."

As Suzanne tensed, her eyes darted to Delia, who studiously avoided looking up by arranging the folds of her floral print silk skirt. Feeling trapped yet knowing she couldn't contradict Vito without hurting his feelings, she merely smiled up at him. "I'm glad you could come."

"How could I possibly miss such a momentous occasion as this?" he countered with one of his boyishly charming smiles as they sat down together on the love seat. "You will only have one twenty-first birthday, *cara mia.*"

The endearment brought a slight frown to Suzanne's brow, but though it vanished almost immediately her anger didn't. At that moment, her palm itched to make contact with her stepmother's smug face. Obviously she had lured Vito over here by telling him an outright lie and now that he believed Suzanne herself had invited him, he apparently thought he had the right to call her *cara mia* since she must be as interested romantically in him as he was in her. To discourage that misconception Suzanne had only gone out to dinner once with him in the three weeks since they had gone with Jared and Angelina to the nightclub, though he had asked her for dates many times. And now all her efforts to simply be his friend had been destroyed simply because Delia had the nerve to interfere in her personal relationships. Suzanne could have happily smacked her, but being a civilized human being, she instead clenched her hands together in her lap and tried to smile graciously at Vito, who was not to blame for any of this. During the meal that followed, she managed to act as if nothing were amiss but the moment Vito left the villa after lunch, she planned to have a frank discussion with her step-mother.

It was nearly two-thirty when Vito declared reluctantly that he must get back to his office in the silk mill. After he had said good-bye to Jack and Delia, Suzanne walked with him through the main gallery and out onto the portico. To her dismay, he kissed her again, his lips lingering against hers this time until she discreetly pulled away from him. He only smiled indulgently. "You *are* a shy little thing, are you not? I did not know exactly how shy until Delia told me you had asked her to invite me for lunch today because you were too bashful to ask me yourself." Shaking his head, he chuckled. "Why are you so timid with me, *cara mia?* I assure you I do not bite. I wish you had spoken to me over the phone last night instead of having Delia tell me that you accepted my invitation to dinner this evening."

Suzanne was too astonished to speak and gazing up at him, her eyes widening, she inadvertently strengthened his belief that she was exceedingly timid. Though she searched desperately for a gentle way to tell him how her stepmother had manipulated both of them, she simply was incapable of diplomacy at the moment. The right words failed to come to mind and when she didn't speak, he caressed her cheek fondly.

"I have bought you a gift for your birthday," he whispered. "But I will give it to you this evening when we can be alone. I will come for you at eight. All right, *cara mia?"*

She was still unable to speak and since he didn't really seem to expect an answer, he squeezed her hand once, then hurried across the portico to the drive where his Ferrari was parked. The top was down and he hopped over the low-slung door into the driver's seat. Then with a jaunty wave, he turned the key in the ignition. With a powerful roar of the engine, he was off down the driveway, his back wheels kicking up a spray of white pebbles behind him.

"Darn it!" Suzanne muttered, then turned and marched back into the gallery. Though she had no idea exactly what she planned to say to Delia, she knew she had to say something, if only to appease the anger building rapidly inside her. Unfortunately, Jack Collins was with his wife when Suzanne stepped into the salon and because he was there perhaps, Delia had the audacity to pretend to smile very innocently at her stepdaughter. "Oh, is Vito gone?" she asked too sweetly, then giggled. "Then I suppose you're ready for me to give you the present I mentioned? Ooh, I just can't wait until you see it; I know you're going to love it." She glanced at her husband and tittered sillily. "You don't mind if I take Suzanne up to my room and give her her present now, do you darling?"

"I was about to go back into my office anyway," Jack said absently, as if he had matters more important than birthday gifts on his mind.

After he had left the salon, Delia ambled over to the double doors where Suzanne stood. Neither of them spoke as they walked up the stairs then along the upper gallery but the moment they were inside the bedroom and the door was closed behind them, Suzanne drew a deep self-controlling breath then proceeded to tell her stepmother what she thought of her meddling.

"Oh, you're getting all in a dither about nothing." Delia snorted indelicately. "You're such a hermit, Suzanne. I had to do something to improve your social life, didn't I?"

"I happen to be perfectly content with my social life," Suzanne answered tersely. "And you had absolutely no right to lie to Vito the way you did. What made you tell him *I* wanted him to come for lunch today and, worse yet, that I wanted to go out to dinner with him this evening?"

"Heavens, I just wanted you to have a pleasant birthday," Delia lied blatantly. "I thought you might enjoy yourself more if you could be with someone near your own age. Besides, what's the big deal? Vito's a wealthy young man. And he's nice too. You could do a lot worse than him, let me tell you."

"I could do a lot worse than him for what?" Suzanne asked sharply. "Just what do you have in mind for Vito and me?"

Holding out her hand, Delia examined her finger-nails and shrugged lazily. "Well, you are getting close to marriageable age, dear. Or maybe you've already passed it."

"I don't care if I have passed it. I'm in no hurry to get married, thank you. And when I decide I'd like to, I intend to choose my future husband myself. I won't let anyone pick him for me."

"Maybe you should let someone guide you then because you seem to be turning your interest in the wrong direction. You have a good chance with a boy like Vito. So why make a fool of yourself by chasing after a man far too sophisticated for you?"

This none-too-subtle reference to Jared both aggra-vated and humiliated Suzanne. Though she knew she didn't chase after him—that in fact, she often avoided him because he made her nervous—she did have to ad-mit to herself that she was more than a little interested in him. Yet, what business was that of Delia's and why did she persist in acting as though she had some claim on him? Unless she were personally involved with him herself, she really shouldn't care if Suzanne found him intriguing.

Watching her stepmother saunter across the room to the mirrored doors of her vast closet, Suzanne sighed inwardly. She had almost reached the point where she could dismiss all the disturbing questions she had once had about Jared and Delia's relationship but her step-mother's possessive attitude toward him today was stirring them all up again. And Suzanne certainly didn't need to have those suspicions rearoused. It disturbed her enough to realize Jared was very likely involved in an intimate relationship with Angelina. She didn't want to be burdened with the horrid worry that he also might be having an affair with her father's wife. Hoping to push all such thoughts far back in her mind, she tried to muster some interest in the large white glossy box Delia removed from the shelf of her closet.

"Well, don't just stand there," Delia commanded, placing the box on her bed. "Come over here and open this."

Without much enthusiasm, Suzanne crossed the room, but before she could reach the bed, the older woman lifted off the top of the box herself. With a flourish, she held up a dress and skimpy was the only word for it. Though it was obviously expensive—of the finest heavy black silk—its design was too provocative to suit Suzanne, even though it was a cocktail dress. The tulip skirt was very narrow; she was certain if she tried it on, it would cling to her hips and thighs, accentuating every feminine contour. That didn't bother her nearly so much as the fact that the V neckline of the dress plunged nearly to the waist. Although Suzanne was slight of build, she had inherited her mother's nicely endowed figure. She was afraid that if she ever dared to wear the dress and made an imprudent move, the intimate details of her figure would be exposed to everyone's view. It was definitely not for her. Because of the fairly generous curve of her breasts, she had always avoided low necklines, even in swimsuits. Surely Delia had noticed that she never wore anything like this.

After staring at the dress for a long time, Suzanne finally spoke. "It's very . . . well, I can see that it's a beautifully made dress but, for me, don't you think it might be too revealing? Personally, I'd rather leave more to the imagination."

"Oh, don't be a prude, darling," Delia said with a careless wave of her hand. "Just think how much older and more sophisticated you would look wearing this."

Suzanne didn't agree with that theory but tried to

keep her tone light. "I really can't see myself in it. A girl with freckles just can't wear a dress like that."

"But dear. . . ."

"No. Really, I think I would look very foolish in it. I'm well aware of the fact that I look younger than I am and I'm afraid if I tried to wear such a sophisticated style, I'd look like a little girl playing dress-up in my mother's clothes." As a guarded look flitted across Delia's face then vanished, Suzanne realized her step-mother agreed with what she had just said. In all probability, she had bought this dress hoping Suzanne would wear it, and consequently make herself look like a juvenile trying to look like a sophisticate. Yet this attempted ploy confused Suzanne. She frowned slightly. "On the flight to Rome, you told me you were tired of me looking younger than I am, that you wished I'd try to look my age. But don't you think this dress would have the opposite effect?"

"I think you just don't like the dress. That's what I think," Delia evaded the question huffily, carelessly stuffing the garment back into the box. "I thought I would please you by buying you something really nice, but since I obviously didn't, you can take the dress back to the shop in Como tomorrow and exchange it for something you think suits you better." She smiled mockingly. "They did have a little blue-checked frock with a white pinafore. Maybe that would be more to your liking."

Refusing to be baited, Suzanne laughed. "I think there must be some middle ground between a black silk cocktail dress and a frock with a pinafore. I'm sure I can find something that I really like."

"Then you'll have to find it without my help," Delia declared truculently, eyes flashing. "Obviously you think I have very poor taste in clothes."

"That's not true," Suzanne answered as patiently as

possible. "You're always fashionably dressed. In fact, this black silk would be perfect for you and I appreciate your buying something you liked for me. But it's just not my style. You understand that."

Flattery mollified Delia slightly. She shrugged. "I was just trying to see that you had something really sophisticated to wear when you go out to dinner with Vito tonight."

Suzanne's shoulders stiffened. Though she was unwilling to argue with her stepmother about a dress, this was a point she had to clarify. Her expression became very serious as she said, "I will go out to dinner with Vito tonight, Delia, but only because I don't want to hurt his feelings by telling him that you deceived him. "But," she added forcibly, "don't try to manipulate me like this again."

"I was only trying to see that you had a nice birthday," Delia lied irritably. "Jared and Angelina are coming here this evening and I didn't think you'd want to stay and be bored by all of us older people. I thought you'd have a much nicer time out with Vito, who's young enough for you."

Suzanne sighed. "Jared and Angelina aren't exactly ancient."

"They're too old for you to socialize with," Delia snapped. "They would bore you and you would certainly bore them."

The very suggestion that Suzanne would ever find Jared Caine boring was laughable but she didn't laugh. Instead, she walked across the room to the closed door, placed her hand on the knob, then turned back toward Delia. "Just don't make any more dates for me," she said flatly. "If I want to see Vito, *I'll* ask him over here or I'll accept his invitations when he asks me to go out with him. Don't interfere. I don't appreciate being pushed off on somebody."

Receiving only another indelicate sniff in answer, Suzanne opened the door, then pulled it closed behind her as she went out. As she walked to her own room, sheer frustration rose in her. Only her concern for her father had prevented her from really telling Delia what she thought of her. Since she didn't want to upset him in any way, she had remained calm but her frustration now demanded some sort of release. In her room, she stripped off her dress and hurriedly slipped into her favorite well-worn cut-off jeans and a comfortably soft off-white knit shirt. After tucking some lire notes into her pocket, she left her room on her way down to the nearest village that overlooked the lake.

Twenty minutes later, she was strolling the narrow winding streets lined with old stone houses, many of which had shops on the ground floor. The homey aroma of freshly baked bread wafted out the open door of a bakery and a table cluttered with plaster statuettes of various saints partially blocked the sidewalk before a souvenir shop. Curious, she went inside, only to discover that the merchandise consisted of handmade straw hats and rayon dresses in bright flowery prints. She wandered back onto the street again, ignoring the admiring glances she received from the men, young and old, that she met as she walked along. Girl-watching was a national pastime and since no disrespect was intended, she had learned to take the blatant stares in stride.

After enjoying a refreshing lemon ice at a miniscule sidewalk cafe, Suzanne walked down to the tiny harbor on the lake. A few fishing vessels were docked there and a small flotilla of sailboats, available for rental. She gazed longingly at the smaller boats. Since her father was not yet up to such strenuous exercise, she hadn't been out on the lake this year and now she realized how much she had missed sailing. She had learned a great deal about sailing from her father, she rationalized. She could think of no reason why she shouldn't be able to handle one of these tiny crafts. On impulse, she approached the man sitting on the edge of the pier, squinting as he disentangled several yards of rope. When she touched his shoulder, he looked up at her and a smile softened the weathered lines of his sun-browned face. When his graying brows lifted questioningly, she pointed toward the smallest boat in the harbor. It had a short mast, and she was sure that even she would be safe in it. When she took the folded lire notes from her pocket, the man understood what she wanted. After she had paid him the required amount, he chivalrously got up and held onto her hand as she stepped down on the flat deck, then sat in the shallow cockpit. He untied the mooring line and she cast off, rowing away from the dock. The fiberglass oars dipped silently into the glittering azure surface of the water.

She stopped rowing and checked her wristwatch. It was now four o'clock so if she sailed for an hour, she would be able to return to the villa with plenty of time to spare before darkness fell. Wind from the north lifted her hair forward over her shoulders and she was glad for the barrettes that kept it secured back from her face. After waving to the man on the pier, she hoisted the sail. It caught the gentle wind, tautened, and the small boat skimmed over the water southward.

It was exhilarating to alter her course merely by maneuvering the tiller and she didn't mind that her shorts and shirt were being thoroughly drenched by the spray. Sailing with the wind was easy; however, after about twenty minutes, Suzanne decided it was time to start back since sailing against the wind meant slow going. Luckily, she discovered she was fairly adept at tacking, zigzagging toward her destination so that she wasn't taken aback by the opposing wind.

She had seen few other boats thus far but now as she sailed past the entrance to a wide cove, she heard the roar of a speedboat approaching from the south. As it ripped past her, she smiled as she saw one bikini-clad girl in the open cockpit seemingly urge the girl at the wheel to increase her speed. They were towing a lone water skier. That intrepid young man—obviously intent on impressing the girls—was skiing barefoot. Suzanne's eyes widened. She knew that some people skied that way occasionally, but she had never actually seen it done. To get a better look at the man's daredevil performance, she knelt on the flat deck. An unexpected gust of easterly wind swung the boom around and as it slammed against her shoulders, she was catapulted into the lake.

When she rose to the surface moments later, her first thought was that she was glad she was wearing a life vest, mainly because it had cushioned the blow from the boom. And she was happy to have it help support her in the water because, although she was a fairly strong swimmer, this surprise dunking had taken her breath away. Her heart was pounding and she was disgusted with herself for making such a foolish error. Yet it wasn't until she started to swim toward the boat that she really realized exactly how much trouble she was in. Gusting winds from every direction were spinning the small craft around and driving it away from her at a speed she couldn't hope to match swimming. She stopped trying to catch it. Treading water, she looked up at the sky and saw immediately why the wind was gusting so crazily. What had been a slightly overcast afternoon sky was now aswirl with dark ominous clouds. A storm was brewing and here she was, overboard in a lake so large she didn't want to think about it right now.

"Fool," she called herself and started swimming.

Luckily, she had noticed a tiny islet of rock centered in the entrance to the cove and it was this refuge she sought. Before she could touch the visible tip of the rock, its sides sloped out beneath the surface so she was able to wade in. Her wet leather sandals squished as she pulled herself up to sit on a rough narrow ledge of the rock. Wrapping her arms around her drawn-up legs, she rested her chin on her knees and tried to think of a way out of her predicament. She looked at the cove. The rock she was on was some distance from any shore but, with the life vest on, she was sure she could have swum in, except she was afraid to. Two mountain streams emptied into the lake along the cove's shoreline and she wondered if they might create dangerous undercurrents. She didn't want to risk finding out.

"So you're stuck here," she muttered aloud, grimacing as she surveyed her ruined sandals. Then she settled back against the rock, waiting for another boat to go by so she could be rescued. Interminable minutes passed and she began to suspect no boat would be passing by. The sky was darkening to a menacing purplish black and any sailor with sense must be making for safe harbor right now. Her throat went dry with the thought that she might be stranded here during the coming storm. She flinched as lightning flashed in the distance and was followed by a low rumble of thunder.

Ten minutes later, the clouds opened, or at least it seemed like it to Suzanne. The storm had gathered force directly overhead. Lashing rain, driven by a chilling wind, poured down. Fierce jagged streaks of lightning flashed on the churning surface of the lake and sharp cracks of thunder exploded in her ears. She covered them with her hands and buried her face in her arms as she huddled on the ledge. Storms had always intrigued her—but then she had always been safely inside during them—until now. Now she was terrified.

On a high point, surrounded by water, she was in a dangerous position. Knowing that lightning could strike at any moment, she vividly felt the powerful and indifferent force of nature. Trembling violently with cold and fear, she pressed herself as close to the rock as she could and waited.

An eternity passed before the thunder and lightning abated and even then the rain still drizzled down, falling in fat plops on her chilled skin. By that time twilight was gathering and darkness was edging in on the lake. Surely the man at the harbor would notice she had never come back in and would send out searchers, she thought frantically, then moaned softly when she realized it still might be hours before they found her here. She might not be found until morning!

Because of her huddled position her legs were beginning to cramp so she stretched them out on the ledge, wincing when the back of her thighs made contact with the cold stone. She was hungry and wet and chilled and she might have cried if she hadn't been so disgusted with herself for getting in this mess in the first place. Then, to add to her misery, she began to worry about her father. He would be so upset when she didn't return to the villa. And if he discovered she had gone sailing and never returned to the harbor, his heart would be put under considerable strain.

Feeling utterly helpless, she leaned her head against the rock and tried to relax. As the time passed slowly, her mind wearied of thinking altogether and she finally drifted into a light dozing sleep.

It was the sound of a boat engine that awakened her. Her eyes flew open and she sat up when she saw the beam of a searchlight moving over the black surface of the water. Desperate to be seen, her heart pounding, she scrambled to her feet, waving her arms and calling out loudly. She could have almost fainted with relief when the beam of light was directed toward the rock on which she was standing and a booming male voice assured her that she had been spotted. There was a moment of panic when the light went out for a moment, leaving her in the darkness once more but it came back on again and she sank down weakly on the ledge to wait.

A few minutes later, she heard the swish of oars gliding through the water. A dinghy moved into the light. Two men were in it and one of them stepped out in about two feet of water and waded toward her. Relief washed over her until she saw that the man was Jared and that the expression on his face was frighteningly grim.

"Are you hurt?" he asked, his voice rough. When she shook her head, he swept her off the ledge into his arms, glaring down at her when she wriggled and insisted she could walk. "Just shut up," he commanded brusquely.

She did. She was docile as a kitten as he lowered her into the dinghy and he and the other man rowed back to the cabin cruiser. Once aboard, she smiled wanly at the boat's owner and his son who had helped row the dinghy. Using as few words as possible, Jared introduced them as Marcello and Nino Marcini and explained that without their help, it might have been morning before she was found. After she had shakily expressed her gratitude to the two men, Jared gripped her hand and impelled her down the companionway stairs into the dimly lighted cabin. His dark eyes roved over her from head to toe in a thorough inspection.

"You're sure you're not hurt?" he nearly growled.

Casting down her eyes, she shook her head and fumbled with the fasteners of her life vest. But her fingers were shaking so violently that she made no progress in undoing them. Finally, with a muffled exclamation, Jared strode to her, brushed her hands away, and removed the vest. As the sound of the engine changed and the boat began moving, she glanced up warily at him. "Is Dad terribly worried?" she whispered "Oh, I hope he isn't."

"He doesn't know you're missing. I told Delia not to tell him," Jared said, his piercing gaze impaling hers. "As far as he knows, you were safe in your room during the storm."

"I wish I had been," she murmured, barely aware that Jared's expression softened slightly. "How . . . did you find me so fast?"

"Pure luck. Lucia saw you walking toward the village. When the storm began, she sent Pietro down to drive you home. He couldn't find you and finally asked Fredo, the man who rented you the boat, if he'd seen a girl fitting your description. Of course he remembered you and that you'd sailed south toward Como. He was concerned because you hadn't returned. Pietro called Delia who called me, in hysterics, naturally. I persuaded her not to tell Jack anything and tried to convince myself you'd reached Como before the storm broke. Unfortunately, before I could get to the village, your boat was found drifting. Marcello was docking in the harbor but agreed to bring me out to search for you. We didn't even know if you could swim and could only hope you had been wearing your life vest."

"I can swim," she said almost inaudibly. "But I'd never sail without wearing a life vest anyway."

With a curt nod, he widened his stance and placed his hands on his hips. "How did you manage to fall overboard?" After she told him very reluctantly, he shook his head and muttered, "Obviously you're no better at sailing than you are at riding a motorbike."

Her eyes darkened with hurt and reproach for that unnecessary remark. "Don't pick on me," she protested weakly, quite unaware of how vulnerable she looked, all bedraggled, her damp clothes clinging to her, her hair tousled. "It's been a rotten day and I don't need you to tell me how inept and clumsy I am." Unable to withstand his critical gaze a moment longer, she glanced at her wristwatch and groaned softly when she saw the water beneath the crystal.

Jared misunderstood her reaction. "Yes, it's nine o'clock so you'll have to postpone your big night out with Vito. But don't worry. I'm sure he'll take you out tomorrow evening."

She shook her head. "I don't care what time it is," she whispered huskily. "It's my watch—it's full of water."

Uttering an explicit curse, Jared gripped her shoulders and shook her. "What is the matter with you? Don't you know you're lucky to be alive right now? How can you be worried about a stupid watch?"

"It was Mother's watch," she muttered thickly. "And now I've ruined it."

Seeing the stricken look on her face, Jared loosened his hold on her and when her chin wobbled slightly and she began to shiver uncontrollably, he relented. "Come here," he commanded softly, pulling her into his arms. "Your skin's like ice and after having pneumonia, this was the last thing you needed to happen to you."

Responding to his sudden kindness, Suzanne offered no resistance when he sat down on the port sofa-bunk and pulled her down onto his lap. As he enfolded her slight trembling body in his arms, she snuggled closer, needing his warmth and the odd sense of security he could evoke in her when he was being nice. The heat that radiated from him began to envelop her. As his lean hand rubbed over her bare arms and even the shapely length of her legs, the friction created by his rougher skin brushing the softness of hers made her

tingle with blessed warmth. Almost of their own voli-
tion, her fingers spread open against his chest, stroking
the muscular contours as she nuzzled her cheek into the
hollow of his shoulder.

"What an enchanting little mess you are," he whispered gently, his breath stirring a tendril of hair that
grazed her temple. As she leaned back her head to look
up at him with drowsy eyes, his lips sought hers, then
trailed soft kisses down to the pulse in her satiny throat.
When her fingers tentatively touched his neck, his
mouth took hers again but with an exquisite tenderness
that somehow conveyed barely leashed passion.

As he cupped the fullness of one breast in a lean
hand and his thumb brushed over the hardening nipple,
a fire blazed to life inside her, dissipating the chill she
had previously felt. Yet as she murmured softly, his
hand dropped down to her waist and his lips released
hers. Her eyes flickered open to search the dark
unfathomable depths of his and her heart skipped
several beats as she suddenly realized that somehow in
the past few weeks, she had foolishly allowed herself to
fall in love with him.

Chapter Seven

"This is a very swanky office, Vito," Suzanne said with a smile. Glancing again at the thick plush beige carpet, the expensive pecan furniture, and the rich patina of the wood-paneled walls, she raised her eyebrows. "I imagine it's fun to work in lush surroundings like this. It must be nice to be a young executive."

"It has its advantages. Many young women are impressed by my position here," he said solemnly, leaning on his hand against the desk, his ankles crossed. "But you are different. *Sì, cara mia?*" You are not at all impressed that I manage an entire silk manufacturing operation, are you?"

"I think it's a notable accomplishment for someone as young as you are," she assured him, then smiled again. "And I know you must be very busy. So I really appreciate your offer to show me around. I can't wait to see how raw silk is made into such beautiful fabric."

"We will begin the tour in a moment. First, I want to discuss us," Vito declared very seriously, walking across the room to where she stood. Taking both her hands in his, he pressed them against his chest. "I understand why you could not go out with me on your birthday but it has been over a week since you were stranded on the lake. Why have you refused every invitation I have made since then? I am beginning to think you do not like me."

"I do like you, Vito. It's just that I'm not ready for a romantic entanglement."

"Ah, then I will have to see what I can do to change your mind." he whispered provocatively, giving her an indulgent smile as she moved back slightly to avoid his attempt to kiss her. With one fingertip, he touched the gold heart-shaped locket that rested in the hollow at the base of her throat. "A birthday gift?"

She nodded, unwilling to tell him the locket had been a completely unexpected gift from Jared, to be worn, he had said, with the chain she had received from her father.

"And since you are not ready for a romance, I suppose you have not put anyone's picture in this locket?" Vito persisted half-teasingly. "Or have you? Shall I open it and see?"

"There's no picture," she lied, covering the locket with her fingers, so he couldn't open it and discover the tiny photograph of Jared. She had found it in the Como newspaper and because Jared had been photographed in a group with several other men, the picture had been small enough to fit in the locket. Yet, even as she had carefully cut it to the required heart shape, she had known there was always a chance someone would open the locket before she could prevent it and discover her secret. But she had let sentiment overrule caution and right now she had to do something to divert Vito's attention. Catching the fingers caressing her neck beneath the gold chain, she gently moved his hand away and hastily said, "Oh, yes, and I want to thank *you* for the perfume you sent me for my birthday."

"But you have already thanked me, *cara mia*. I received your note."

"Oh, well, I just wanted to thank you in person too," she explained, then glanced toward the door. "Perhaps we should start on that tour. I don't want to keep you away from your work too long."

"To be with you, I would gladly forsake my work forever," he proclaimed dramatically then laughed with her as they left his office.

During the two hours that followed, Suzanne learned the rudiments of silk manufacturing. She saw how raw silk was cleaned then twisted into heavier strands for winding on bobbins. Vito showed her the vast airy room where the yarn was woven on huge looms, then they visited the dyeing and printing rooms, where the silk really came to life in a myriad of colors and designs.

"We process millions of yards of silk here every year," Vito told her proudly. "And it is all of the very highest quality, I assure you."

"It's a fascinating process," Suzanne said sincerely. "But you haven't shown me the design department. I mean, where the designs are actually created on paper. Could we go there or are your designs so top secret that you don't allow visitors in that department?"

Vito laughed. "As you know, that department is run by Angel and she can be very secretive, but I think we can trust you not to be an industrial spy. After all, it is your father's corporation that owns the controlling interest in this firm." Grinning broadly, he draped his arm around her shoulders. "So come along. We shall see if Angel will allow us to invade her domain for awhile."

The design department was located back in the office complex. Cork tiled floors muffled their footsteps as they walked down a long narrow corridor on the third floor. Through swinging glass doors they entered a vast room, bright with sunlight. The room had a southern exposure and the entire outer wall consisted of great panes of glass.

"This looks like one of those modern office buildings back in the States," Suzanne said softly. "All glass and not much else."

"This was one of Jared's innovations," Vito answered. "He says designers are artists and artists need light to work." Cupping her elbow, he guided her down the aisle between two rows of high slanted-top worktables then stopped beside a young man who was sitting sideways on a high stool, chewing thoughtfully on one end of his drawing pencil. As he glanced up and saw Vito, he began speaking in rapid Italian, waving his hands expressively. When Vito patted his shoulder and spoke in much calmer tones, he settled back on his stool with a nod and a sigh and recommenced chewing the pencil.

"Something wrong?" Suzanne inquired as she and Vito moved on. "He seemed upset."

Vito spread his hands in a resigned gesture. "Santino is our best designer. He becomes very involved in his work. When it is not going as well as he would like it to sometimes, he does get upset but we do not mind humoring him because his designs are excellent and very original."

All the designers were Italian and Suzanne and Vito stopped to chat with most of them as they strolled the aisles between the rows of worktables. At the end of the last two rows there was a long, glass-partitioned cubicle, made private by closed venetian blinds. Vito rapped once on the door, then indicated Suzanne should precede him into the office.

She did so but with extreme reluctance. As they entered the office, Angelina Sorveno looked up from the papers on her desk and the expression that hardened her face was far from welcoming. Her cold gaze flicked over Suzanne for an instant before she turned an impatient glare on Vito and folded her hands together on top of her desk with a sigh. When she spoke, it was in Italian.

Vito, however, answered in English. "Surely you are not too busy to spare us a few minutes, Angel. Jack asked me to give Suzanne a tour of the mill and since she is most interested in the design department, I knew she would enjoy speaking to you."

Before Angelina could comment, the ornate phone on her desk rang. After answering it, she listened without speaking for a few seconds, then replaced the receiver. "The maintenance supervisor is on his way here to talk to you," she informed Vito. "Something about a problem with one of the looms. It is urgent, he says."

Vito grimaced regretfully as he turned to Suzanne. *"Scusa, cara mia,* but I must leave you for a moment. But while I go discuss this problem, you stay here with Angelina and she will gladly answer your questions about her department. I will return immediately."

As he dashed away, Suzanne smiled apologetically at the older girl. "I understand you're too busy to answer questions right now, so I won't bother you with any. But if it's all right, I'll just sit down here and wait for Vito."

"Yes, do sit down," Angelina responded curtly, opening one drawer of her desk. "I have something to return to you anyway. I had planned to send it to your father by messenger but since you are here now. . . ." With an impertinent flick of her wrist, she tossed a folded sheet of drawing paper toward Suzanne. "It will not be possible for us to use this."

Rather confused, Suzanne retrieved the paper from the floor where it had fallen. Unfolding it, she discovered it was the royal blue and tan swirl design she had drawn and shown to her father. Obviously, despite her request that he not give the design to Jared, he had done so anyway and Jared had passed it on to Angelina. Suzanne felt vaguely embarrassed as she refolded the paper and glanced up at the older girl. "I suppose Jared gave this to you?"

"Jared? No, of course not. Your father sent it to me," Angelina replied with a haughty shrug. "He thought it would be a suitable design for a scarf but I cannot use it."

"Dad mentioned that he might show this to Jared so I assumed—"

"Jared does not try to do my job for me," Angelina interrupted with a smug uncurling of her lips. "He and I, we have an understanding—in business as well as personal matters. He would never demand that I use a design simply because it was created by a relative of his."

Suzanne's eyes widened. "Are you saying my father demanded you use this design because it was mine?"

"Well, no, he did not demand I use it," Angelina conceded, looking away rather uncomfortably. "He only suggested." As she straightened the collar of her tailored gray blouse, she regained her former haughty expression. "Perhaps your father does not understand that I never use the work of amateurs. I have only the very best professionals in my department and I use only *their* best efforts. Jared gives me complete authority." She smiled suggestively. "I mean, here in this department, I have complete authority. My personal relationship with Jared is different. He is one of those incredibly masculine men who can persuade any woman to do his bidding. I would never think of denying Jared anything he asked of me."

Angelina's insinuating little laugh made Suzanne feel ill. Though she had suspected Jared's relationship with her might be intimate, Suzanne had no masochistic desire to hear any of the details Angelina seemed so eager to share. Attempting to show no reaction at all to the older girl's provocative declaration, she forced a bland smile. "I'm sorry if you got the impression that Dad meant for you to use my design. I'm sure he only wanted you to consider it but since you don't like it. . . ."

"It is not a very good design," Angelina said bluntly, adjusting the lapels of the jacket of her charcoal gray pantsuit. "There is a certain originality to the swirl pattern but I decided it simply would not do for a scarf."

"I understand," Suzanne replied tonelessly. "I'm sure you know much more about design than I do."

"I have been told that I have impeccable taste," Angelina boasted, admiring her crimson-polished fingernails. "And I do not think your design would make a very pretty scarf. I just do not like it."

"What is it you do not like?" Vito asked, catching her last few words as he stepped back into the office. After smiling at Suzanne, he turned to Angelina, his expression questioning. "What are you two lovely ladies discussing?"

The older girl tossed her hand in a dismissive gesture. "It was nothing of importance—only a design Signorina Collins had done. Her father sent it over to me but, in my opinion, it would not be suitable to use as a design for one of our scarves, as he suggested. I did not like the drawing at all."

Frowning, Vito held out his hand. "I would like to see the design."

Shrugging, Angelina inclined her head toward Suzanne. "I returned it to her."

His hand still outstretched, Vito turned to the younger girl, his expression softening. "Let me see your drawing, *cara*." After she handed him the folded paper with some reluctance, he opened it and began immediately to nod his head. "But this is quite lovely, Angel. I cannot see what objections you could have to it. I think it would make a lovely scarf design."

"I cannot agree," Angelina retorted, angry color rising in her cheeks. "The color combination of royal blue and tan is not attractive."

"That is your opinion," Vito countered determinedly. "I think the colors are very attractive together. Besides, it is the pattern that is important. Any colors could be used: black on white, white on black, scarlet on gray—the possibilities are endless."

"The pattern is not to my liking either," the woman said heatedly, brown eyes beginning to glitter. "All those swirls make it look like a child's figerpainting."

"You are wrong. It is a beautiful swirl pattern."

"It shows it is the work of an amateur."

"It shows talent," Vito argued, his own temper rising. "This time, Angel, I think you are totally wrong in your opinion. And I want this design to be used."

"I make the decisions in this department!" Angelina exclaimed furiously, rising quickly to her feet behind her desk. "I have complete authority here! I will not allow you to tell me which designs I will use."

"You seem to be forgetting that I am your superior," Vito countered sharply. "I am the manager of this firm; you are merely a department supervisor and when I tell you to do something—"

"Vito, please, this is all unnecessary," Suzanne interceded hastily, hating to be the center of this controversy. "I never meant for my design to cause all this trouble. Actually, I only drew it for my own personal use. It was Dad's idea to send it over here. Really, if Angelina doesn't want to use it, it's not important."

"It is important to me," he declared hotly, still

glaring at the older girl. "Imaginative designs are not easy to come by and I see no reason why this one should be discarded simply because you, Angel, are not judging it objectively."

Angelina laughed nastily. "*I* am not judging it objectively! Hah! That is ridiculous! *You* are the one who is not being objective." She shot a disgusted glance toward Suzanne. "It is this girl you think is so wonderful, not her amateurish design and I refuse to allow you to use me and my department just to give her what she wants."

As Vito snarled back at her and the argument lapsed into virulent exchanges in Italian, Suzanne stood, touching his arm as she tried to persuade him that it didn't matter to her whether her design was used or not. But her softly spoken words weren't even heard as the argument quickly disintegrated into a shouting match. Fortunately, as Vito's voice became louder and Angelina's became shriller, Jared opened the door and stepped into the office. Unnoticed for a moment, except by Suzanne who instinctively went to stand near him, he folded his arms across his chest and watched the two combatants for several seconds. Finally, he remarked laconically, "I presume the two of you are having a little difference of opinion?"

Though he had not raised his voice in the slightest, the argument immediately ceased. Both the man and woman spun around to stare at him but while Vito appeared a bit embarrassed at being caught bickering, Angelina simply changed her entire personality. As she ran her fingers through her raven hair, reproach darkened her eyes and she allowed her lips to tremble slightly.

"It is nothing, Jared," she said, taking on the role of brave little woman, her voice no longer strident. "Vito was merely reminding me that he is my superior. I-I had thought I had total authority in this department but. . . ."

As Vito snorted disgustedly and started to interrupt, Jared silenced both of them by lifting up one hand. "Would either of you like to tell me what this argument is about?"

When Vito began to explain the situation, then handed Jared Suzanne's design, her cheeks reddened with chagrin. She had never wanted Jared to even see her drawing. Although Angelina's criticism hadn't bothered her one whit, she knew she would not be able to shrug off an unfavorable opinion from Jared so easily. What if he hated her design? As he looked at it for what seemed an eternity of time, she held her breath. Ignoring Vito and Angelina, he at last turned to Suzanne. The color in her cheeks deepened to dusky rose as she searched his lean brown face for some clue as to what he thought of the drawing. His expression told her nothing.

"Very attractive," he said finally. "I like it."

"Do you really?" she breathed, his approval making her unreasonably happy. "Are you sure?"

"I'm sure," he answered, his voice low. A glint of amused indulgence danced in his brown eyes as he looked down into her uplifted face. For a spellbinding moment, it was as if they were alone in the office until Vito's voice intruded.

"You see, Angel," he crowed triumphantly. "Jared likes the design too. Now you have to agree to use it."

"I do not have to agree to anything!" she protested vehemently, anger overriding her desire to evoke Jared's sympathetic support. "This is my department and I make the decisions here!"

"Enough," Jared commanded before Vito could voice a retort. "Maybe I'd better clarify my position. I do like the design but I have no intention of becoming involved in this argument. When the corporation bought the controlling interest in this firm, Jack and I had no desire to start making simple, routine decisions, such as this one. You're the manager of the entire operation, Vito, but Angelina is the head of this department. You can order her to use Suzanne's design, of course, but I'd suggest the two of you search for a more amicable solution to the problem."

"I refuse to use her silly little design, Jared," Angelina snapped, obviously displeased that he had not supported her wholeheartedly. "I hate it, it is ugly and I will not use it. That is my final word."

"You are acting like a shrew!" Vito declared. "The design is not ugly and you know it."

The battle recommenced, once again in heated Italian but Jared only shook his head, then without warning reached for Suzanne's hand and took her with him as he exited the office. "That argument could go on for quite some time and I assume you have no desire to witness it. Do you?" When she shook her head, he guided her out of the design department across the corridor to the elevators. "We'll go up to my office," he said as the elevator doors swished open and they stepped inside. "I have your watch. The jeweler finished the repairs early and delivered it to me today."

Suzanne smiled gratefully at him. "I'll be glad to have it back. I've missed it. It was kind of you to see to it that the repairs were done so quickly. Thank you."

His only response was a slight smile as the elevator stopped on the fourth floor and they stepped out into the reception area of the corporate offices. Years ago, before the mill had been constructed next door, the office building had been a small exclusive hotel and the fourth floor had been restored to its former beauty. The marble tiled floors gleamed and the frescoed walls in their faded glory had not been covered over with sterile wood paneling. Both Jared's secretary's office and his own were devoid of plush carpeting and typically modern furniture. His office was a large rectangular room, its ceiling supported at intervals by two rows of slender fluted marble columns. Two small settees and a few chairs were covered with dark blue and cream tapestry. His large teakwood desk sat at the far end of the room; behind it, French doors opened onto a balcony.

As Jared released Suzanne's elbow and went on to his desk, she stopped beside one of the columns, unable to prevent herself from watching him. He wore no coat and the vest of his gray pin-striped suit was unbuttoned. His burgandy tie was slightly loosened at the collar and the long sleeves of his white shirt were rolled up to his elbows, exposing muscular forearms covered with fine dark hair. She was forced to suppress an incredibly urgent desire to touch him but allowed her fascinated gaze to follow his lean brown hands as he opened a desk drawer and removed a box covered in black velvet.

As he turned to come back to her, she tried to ignore the erratic beating of her heart, wanting desperately to appear calm and sophisticated. Yet when he stopped within touching distance, then allowed his gaze to travel slowly over her as he gave one of those warm nearly irresistible smiles, all her hope of remaining cool and blasé vanished. As she detected the spicy fragrance of his aftershave, she longed to move toward him, to feel his strong arms catch her slender body up close against the powerful hardness of his. She looked up at him through the dark fringe of her lashes, then lifted her head to meet his dark gaze directly. Her green eyes became softly lambent and perhaps the discernible radiance in their depths revealed some of what she was feeling because he put out one hand as if to touch her.

"Suzanne," he murmured, his deep voice endearingly husky. Then he shook his head with a sigh and instead of touching her face, he lifted the gold locket that was nestled in the hollow at the base of her throat.

She was so afraid he might open it and find his picture inside that her heart stopped beating for a moment but when he only continued to hold it, she was able to breathe again, though not quite normally. His hard knuckles were grazing her collarbone, evoking a throbbing response deep inside her. All her fears about his relationships with both Delia and Angelina were temporarily vanquished by an intense desire to which she surrendered. Her small hands trembled as they cupped his lean face and she gave a murmur of satisfaction as her fingertips traced the fascinating indentations in his cheeks beside his mouth.

Passion glinted in his black eyes. With a rough whispering of her name, he pocketed the velvet box, and pulled her to him. One arm encircled her waist. One hand tangled in the silky thickness of her hair, tilting her head back as he sought her mouth. He kissed her many times and with increasing thoroughness. His hands moving over the firm mounds of her breasts, then following her curving waist and the gentle outward swell of her hips sent her senses spiraling. Warm, soft, acquiescent, she pressed closer to his lean strength, her hands massaging the taut muscles of his shoulders as her eager lips parted wider beneath the power of his. As his hands slipped down to curve around her upper thighs and press her closer still against his dangerous hardness, she took a sharp half-startled breath.

With a tortured groan, Jared released her lips. "You foolish child. What do you expect?" he muttered, gently pulling her hands from his shoulders and holding her away from him. He examined her delicate features intently, a hot glow still smouldering in his black eyes.

"I told you once that I'm not a boy you can play games with. Don't make me want you too much, Suzanne."

"Why not?" she breathed.

"You don't know what you're saying," he muttered gruffly, then took the box from his pocket and thrust it into her hand. "Take your watch and go find Vito."

"I don't want to find Vito," she murmured, opening the box, removing the gold watch, then giving it to him. "Would you put it on me, please?"

The angular planes of his lean face hardened as he buckled the gold mesh watchband around her small wrist, but when she reached up with her free hand to touch the dark thickness of his hair, she heard his sharply drawn breath. "You're crazy, do you know that," he whispered even as he lifted her hand to his mouth and his lips sought the sensitive palm. "Suzanne, I—"

His words were halted by a knock on the door and when Vito entered the office a second later, he frowned. Though Jared had pulled Suzanne's hand down, he hadn't yet released it and even when he did, Vito's frown didn't disappear. "I have been looking for both of you."

"Suzanne came up to get her watch. I had a jeweler repair it for her," Jared explained coolly. Thrusting his hands into his pockets, he sat down on the edge of his desk, his long legs outstretched in front of him as he gazed steadily at the younger man. "Did you and Angel settle your differences?"

"Yes," Vito answered curtly. "Suzanne's design will be used. I insisted." When she opened her mouth to protest, he gave her no chance to speak. "You promised to have lunch with me, remember? Shall we go now?"

Suzanne's still bemused green eyes sought Jared's face but his expression was beyond analysis. Finally she turned to Vito and nodded. Since she had promised to have lunch with him, she could hardly refuse to go with him now. "I'm ready," she said softly, "whenever you are."

"Let's go then," he muttered, wasting no time opening the office door for her. Before she could do more than glance back over her shoulder at Jared, Vito rushed her through the secretary's office, across the reception area to the elevators. As they waited for the doors to open, he gripped her elbow and turned her to him. "I have always noticed that Jared is very protective with you," he said rather grimly. "Now, I am beginning to wonder why."

Suzanne met his probing gaze directly. "I don't know what you mean."

"Yes, you do," Vito replied harshly as he shook his head. "Perhaps you do not need this warning but I will give it anyway. He is not for you, Suzanne. He has women like Angel in his life. You could get hurt very badly. Just remember that."

As if she could forget that fact, she thought bleakly. Yet as she stepped into the elevator with Vito a second later, she began to resign herself to another hard fact—love didn't die simply because common sense and an instinct for self-preservation said it should. Her feelings for Jared had already grown too strong to die an easy or painless death.

Chapter Eight

Suzanne was unusually restless. All her thoughts centered on Jared lately, making it impossible to concentrate enough to read or do anything else. Even the long walks she had previously enjoyed now allowed her too much opportunity to think about him, especially since her thoughts were so confusing. Common sense told her she should avoid Jared. If she didn't see him, she wouldn't risk being swept into an intimate involvement that to him would be nothing more than a casual affair. Yet, sometimes she longed to see him so badly that she wondered if something—anything—wouldn't be better than nothing at all. At times she found it unbearable to think of returning to Vermont in the fall with nothing but the memory of a few brief kisses to remind her of the man she loved. Yet, she also knew a summer affair would never be enough for her. She would want Jared to return her love and since he couldn't, she would be irrevocably hurt.

With such a conflict whirling around in her head, she often found herself wandering through the villa, seeking something to do that would effectively divert her thoughts. On Thursday, three days after the scene in his office, she decided to give up the idea of batiking curtains for her apartment in Vermont. Instead she had driven into Como and purchased several yards of pomegranate-colored openweave fabric, choosing that bright color to enliven the living room with its rather dull brown tweed furniture. Using Lucia's sewing machine, she had finished the project by early evening, leaving her once again feeling restless.

In her room, she tried to read for awhile but even the entertaining family saga she had begun yesterday couldn't hold her interest. With a sigh she closed the book, tucked her bare feet up beside her in the chair, and rested her head back against the cushion. As she glanced around the room, her gaze fell on the curtains, lying neatly folded on her bed. Sitting up straight, she stared pensively at them. Perhaps instead of mailing them to Lynn as she had intended, she should just go back to Vermont now and take them with her. It would probably be wise to leave Italy before she became any more involved with Jared than she already was. Yet, she wasn't at all certain she could willingly leave him.

She left the chair to pace the floor for several minutes and made a difficult decision. Before she lost her nerve or changed her mind, she went downstairs to see her father. Luckily, she found him alone. He was in the salon mixing before-dinner drinks when she entered and she stopped in the doorway for a moment to observe him. He was looking much healthier now than he had when she had arrived in Como, and his doctor was allowing him to go down to the corporate offices and work two or three hours a day. Tonight, he looked quite handsome in a navy blazer and white turtleneck sweater but as Suzanne watched him, a nostalgic sadness overtook her. Before her mother had died, there had always been a sparkle of genuine happiness in his eyes but that sparkle was never there anymore. He was still a man of boundless energy, yet some of his former enthusiasm for life was missing. Suzanne knew she couldn't help him regain what he had lost, and since he seemed reasonably content with Delia he really didn't need his daughter. Still, Suzanne approached him with a certain amount of dread. It wasn't going to be easy to tell him her decision.

"Dad, I'd like to talk to you," she spoke up intently, wishing she didn't feel so nervous about speaking to her own father. "Is now a good time?"

Turning from the bar toward her, Jack nodded. "Sure, now's as good a time as any. What is it you want to talk about?"

Encouraged, she was able to relax a bit as she walked across the room to him. When he offered her a glass of white wine, she declined and when he had finished making his own drink, they sat down together on the sofa. After taking a sip of his drink, he looked at her questioningly, obviously expecting her to start the conversation.

"Dad, I'm thinking of going back home," she began abruptly, clasping her hands together in her lap. "I've been here over six weeks and since you're feeling better, I think it's time for me to go." She tried to smile teasingly. "I don't want to wear out my welcome, you know."

"What nonsense!" he responded grumpily, apparently in no mood to hear flippant remarks. "You know you're welcome to stay here as long as you like. And I assumed you considered *this* your home since it's where I live, but obviously I was wrong. You call that tiny apartment home."

Suzanne gestured uncertainly. "I guess I said it that way because the apartment is where I've lived for over two years. Lynn and I always speak of it as home."

"Home is where your family is," her father reminded her pithily. "Lynn has a real home with her family and you have a real one here with me. And I see no reason why you should leave yet. August has barely begun.

You still have three or four weeks before school starts again. So why are you so eager to go?"

She couldn't answer that question because she *wasn't* eager to go. She didn't want to leave him—or Jared. She simply thought she ought to.

Detecting her lack of firm resolve, Jack took one of her hands between both his and patted it gently. "You'll stay the rest of the summer," he declared, then followed his command with a hopeful smile. "Won't you? Delia and I will be socializing more now that my doctor's no longer keeping me on a tight rein so you shouldn't be so bored."

"Oh, I'm not bored, I assure you," she said, smiling ruefully. How could she possibly be bored when her emotions were constantly aroused to a fever pitch because she knew Jared was never far away and might show up at the villa at any given moment. No, being in love certainly wasn't conducive to boredom and she shook her head at her father. "Really, I'm never bored so don't think you and Delia have to socialize more just to keep me occupied. It isn't necessary."

Jack grimaced comically. "Well, to tell the truth, Delia has our social calendar pretty much filled anyway. Unfortunately, few if any of our acquaintances have children your age." Releasing Suzanne's hand, he picked up his drink again to take a sip. "Too bad you aren't interested in Vito. If you two could have gotten a romance going, you might have married him and stayed here permanently."

Regarding him intently, Suzanne tilted her head to one side. "You almost sound as if you'd like for me to stay here."

He frowned. "Why does that surprise you? *You* sound as if you think I don't care anything about you."

Intrinsically honest, she had to tell the truth. "We

aren't very close anymore, Dad. We haven't really been since Mother—"

"As children grow up, they naturally begin to drift away from their parents," he interrupted gruffly. "That's just the way it is."

He was trying to shut her out again and this time, she couldn't allow it. "Maybe you just won't let yourself be close to me anymore," she suggested softly. "Is it because I look like Mother? Does seeing me make you miss her even more?"

Jack went a bit pale beneath his tan and pain darkened his blue eyes. But he shook his head. "Your resemblance to Katherine has nothing to do with us. We simply can't be as close as we were when you were twelve because now you're an adult."

But does that mean we have to be strangers? Suzanne started to ask, then changed her mind. He might deny that her resemblance to her mother didn't bother him but she had seen the truth in his face when she had asked the question. Her shoulders drooped slightly. Their problem seemed unsolvable. She would always look like her mother so he would never be able to be close to her again. Suppressing a sigh, she stared down at her feet, feeling a great pity for her father yet also feeling rejected by him. She certainly didn't know what to say to him at the moment and since he seemed disinclined to talk, she finally stood. "I think I'll go up to my room and read awhile before dinner."

"But you have decided to stay here for a few more weeks?" he asked, rising to his feet also. "Haven't you? You will stay?"

The urgency in his voice brought a new understanding to Suzanne. He wanted her close but not too close. He still loved her, yet he could no longer allow himself to express how he felt. But now, as long as she knew the love was there, she would be able to accept the fact that he hid it. If he needed her to stay for a few more weeks, she didn't see how she could refuse. At last she nodded, "I'll stay."

Relief was visible in his expression for a fleeting moment and he nodded. "Good. That's good. Well, now that that's settled, I have a suggestion to make. You mentioned inviting Lynn over here for a week or two and I think you should. I'll even pay her plane fare."

Lynn and her carefree approach to life was exactly what Suzanne needed right now and her father's suggestion pleased her. On impulse, she hugged him. "Thank you, Dad."

Kissing her cheek, he laughed and surprised her by saying, "You're a sweet child."

She grinned at him. "I thought I was an adult now, so how can you say I'm a sweet *child.*"

"Because sometimes when you're excited you still look like you're twelve," he retorted, then walked away to the bar to refresh his drink.

Before Suzanne could think of a snappy answer to his remark, Lucia appeared in the doorway. "Is the telephone call for you, *signorina,*" she announced softly. "Is Signore Gallio, I believe."

"Ah, so Vito hasn't given up, has he?" Jack called as Suzanne excused herself and started to leave the room. "Why don't you take pity on that young man this one time? Agree to go out with him."

"You're assuming he's going to ask me out," she shot back over her shoulder as she walked out the door. She crossed the gallery and entered the small salon where Lucia said she had taken the call. She paused momentarily to look at the white phone on the glass tabletop, then took a deep breath as she picked up the receiver. She wasn't really expecting Vito to be very friendly. In fact, she was surprised he had called at all. After he had correctly assessed her feelings for Jared that day she had toured the mill, he hadn't been very talkative when they had gone on to have lunch together. Wondering what he wanted now, she said hello rather hesitantly, then breathed a silent sigh of relief when he responded in a friendly voice.

After they exchanged pleasantries, however, Vito's tone lowered and became much more serious. "I owe you an apology," he insisted. "I have been thinking about the warning I gave you the other day and I realized that perhaps I jumped to a wrong conclusion. I told you Jared could hurt you very badly but you never actually said you are romantically involved with him. Could it be that I only imagined that you are?"

Inherent honesty once again prevented her from telling a lie. "It's not your imagination," she replied quietly. "I . . . care for Jared but don't assume that means he cares for me because he doesn't."

For a few tense seconds, there was silence on the line, then Vito said very kindly, "I think perhaps you need a friend. May I apply for the position?"

Suzanne laughed softly with relief. "I've always considered you my friend and yes, I do need one. Doesn't everyone who suffers from a case of unrequited love?"

"So it is that bad, hmm? And you are certain your love is unrequited?"

"Absolutely certain. Men rarely fall in love with ingenues like me when sophisticates like Angelina are chasing after them. You told me that yourself."

"I had a selfish motive for saying that," Vito confessed. "I didn't want you to be interested in Jared."

"No matter what your motive was, what you said was true. Jared couldn't be interested in a little thing like me," Suzanne retorted, though her attempt at flippancy didn't succeed. "I can't possibly compete with women like Angelina."

"But as I have mentioned before, Jared is very protective where you are concerned—too protective, I think, for a man you say cares nothing for you."

"Maybe he just feels responsible for me," Suzanne said dully. "You know, because he's Dad's partner and Dad's been sick. Jared's always making remarks about how young I am so I guess he thinks I need someone to watch over me, to see I don't get into trouble." Now thoroughly depressed, she sank down on the armless overstuffed white chair beside the glass and chrome table. "Why don't we talk about something else? This discussion is pointless."

"All right, if you wish. I *do* have some good news for you. Your design will be photochemically stenciled tomorrow and in a few weeks it will be on some of our finest silk scarves. Does that make you feel more cheerful?"

"It's very gratifying," she replied sincerely. "But I still regret being the cause of an argument between you and Angelina. Maybe you shouldn't have insisted she use the design. I'm sure she's very upset with you."

"So?" Vito quipped blithely. "Angelina needs to be reminded occasionally that she is not the manager of the entire firm—I am. And since this is the first time I have ever overruled her, she had better begin to appreciate the nearly unlimited authority she has in design. Managers in some other silk firms I know would never give anyone as much authority as she has now."

"In other words, you're the fairest boss she's likely to find, right? Well, Dad did tell me the mill employees are treated well."

"Yes, Jared insists we try to make them happy. He says we will keep the best workers that way," Vito declared, then paused for a few seconds. "I apologize, Suzanne. I did not mean to mention Jared again."

She had to laugh. "Heavens, I'm not so lovesick that I can't bear to hear his name. But, enough of that. Let me tell you about my friend, Lynn. I'm going to invite her for a visit and if she is able to come, I think you'd like to meet her. She's very pretty."

Vito's interest was piqued. For the remainder of their conversation, Suzanne answered questions about Lynn, which she was happy to do. She liked Vito and was relieved his romantic interest in her hadn't really been very serious. Now they could simply be friends and after they said their good-byes, she was feeling somewhat less alone than she had before he had called.

Deciding she had time before dinner to write to Lynn, Suzanne left the small salon, then stopped short in the gallery as she saw Jared leaving her father's study. Simply seeing him so unexpectedly was enough to make her legs suddenly go weak—a sensation that intensified considerably when he glanced up and saw her standing there watching him. As he strode across the gallery, she tensed, recalling in vivid detail their last meeting and wondering if he was remembering too. Hopefully not. She had behaved almost wantonly and now, as he stopped before her, she had to compel herself to smile up at him.

Disturbingly, he didn't return the smile. Instead, his eyes narrowed and surveyed her face with such an intense scrutiny that she actually ceased breathing for a long tense moment. "You look upset," he said abruptly. "So did Jack. What's wrong?"

Releasing her breath in a sigh, she lifted one hand in a resigned gesture. "We finally talked about my mother. And although he didn't actually admit it, I'm sure you're right about his feelings. I do remind him of her and . . . well, I think that's why it's difficult for him to be close to me anymore."

"I see," Jared murmured, his gaze darkening. "And can you accept how he feels?"

"I don't really have much choice, do I?" she tried to answer nonchalantly but was unable to control the revealing catch in her voice. As she bent her head and stared pensively at his shirtfront, she lifted her shoulders in a slight shrug. "Oh, well, now at least I understand his aloof attitude. That helps a little."

"But not much."

"No, not much."

Jared put out one hand as if he meant to touch her, then changed his mind and slipped his lean long fingers into the pocket of his trousers. "Jack said you were on the phone with Vito. I suppose you two have plans for this evening."

A tiny smile lifted the corners of Suzanne's softly curved lips as she shook her head. "No, he just called to chat. But what about you? Will you be staying for dinner with us?"

"Not tonight. I told Maria, my housekeeper, I'd be home for dinner." Jared glanced down at the thin gold watch around his wrist. "In fact, I'd better be going now. It's nearly eight and I planned to have a swim before dinner."

Suzanne's eyes swept up to meet his and unwittingly conveyed a longing in their soft green depths. "It is a lovely night for a swim—warm, moonlit." She smiled. "I'm going to have to try to convince Dad to have a pool installed here."

Jared simply looked down at her for several long seconds, then his jaw tautened as he commanded brusquely, "Go get a swimsuit and a dress. You'll have dinner with me after our swim."

Pride stiffened Suzanne's shoulders. She thrust out

her small chin rather defiantly as she shook her head. "I wasn't fishing for an invitation, Jared. I merely said. . . ."

"I know what you said. Now, go get a swimsuit. Even if you had been fishing for an invitation, I wouldn't have asked you to join me if I hadn't wanted to—so stop being obstinate and go get your suit."

She hesitated only an instant before the desire to go with him overwhelmed all other considerations. "I'll be right back," she said softly, stepping around him to rush up the stairs.

Ten minutes later, they were at Jared's villa. After he parked the Jaguar in the large garage, they walked across the flagstone courtyard and down a short flight of marble steps. They followed a walkway that circumvented the gardens and led to the large oval swimming pool. Suzanne had only seen a glimpse of it when Jared had shown her the grounds a few weeks ago and now she was rather glad she hadn't first seen it in the daytime. Moonlight shimmered on the colonnades erected at each end of the pool and sparkled on the smooth surface of the clear water. Even the gentle breeze that stirred the air tonight was unusually warm so the pool looked infinitely inviting. There was only one problem. Suzanne didn't exactly relish the idea of changing to her swimsuit in the surrounding shrubbery.

As she should have known, the facilities weren't nearly so primitive. Jared directed her toward the colonnade at the far end of the pool which led to a small white building tucked secludedly in a circle of fir trees. There were two arched entrances and he escorted her to the one on the right, opened the door, then leaned inside to switch on the light. "Meet you at the pool," he said as she walked into the bathhouse.

After closing the door behind her, Suzanne stood still, rather in awe of the luxurious accommodations.

This wasn't a typical, somewhat dilapidated bathhouse. There was a veined marble floor instead of wooden boarding and a mirror covered the entire length of one side wall. The remaining walls were plastered and decorated with reproductions of famous paintings. Unbuttoning her shirt, she walked past two wrought iron dressing tables and their matching chairs, which actually sported red velvet cushions. A sofa covered with some synthetic fabric she hoped was water resistant sat against the plastered side wall and beyond it was a closet with double louvered doors. It was stocked with wooden hangers, and she made use of one and hung up both her shirt and denim skirt. She put her underclothes in one of the built-in drawers, then slipped her forest green maillot swimsuit on. After plaiting her hair into one fat braid, she secured it with an elastic band and put on a short white terry cloth beach robe.

When she went outside to the pool, Jared was already there, muscularly lean and lithe in white swimming trunks. Suzanne tried not to stare at him but it was difficult not to. She had never seen him before in such a state of undress. If she had she might not have agreed to come tonight. His skin was bronze in the moonlight and the powerful lineation of his long body was sensuous and frankly intimidating. Wrapping her beach robe closer around her, she smiled weakly as he watched her approach.

"I'm impressed," she said, her voice too squeaky. "That's some bathhouse. I wish my apartment looked that good."

He smiled. "The bathhouse is a legacy left by the former owner. Needless to say he had more opulent taste than I do."

"It is a bit too fancy, isn't it? I'll hate to go back in there all dripping wet after our swim." Standing on the edge of the pool's tiled apron, she gazed down at the water. "That looks so cool. It's been hot today, don't you think? It must be nice to have your very own pool for warm evenings like this."

"You're welcome to come over anytime you want a swim," Jared offered. "During the day, you'd have it all to yourself. It would be something to do when you get really bored."

Detecting a censuring note in his voice, she looked up at him. "I rarely get bored."

"Jack thinks you do. He thinks that's why you mentioned going back to Vermont."

"Well, it isn't," Suzanne murmured, still gazing down at the water. "Boredom had nothing to do with my suggestion that I should go home."

"You just never wanted to come in the first place, did you?" Jared inquired tersely. "Even though Jack was ill and wanted to see you, Delia had to beg you to come."

Suzanne spun around, her eyes darting up to meet his. "Did she tell you that?" she gasped. "And you believed her?"

"Why shouldn't I?"

"Because it's a lie! She tried her best to persuade me *not* to come but I insisted!" Anger flared in Suzanne's eyes and incautiously loosened her tongue. "What is it with you two? Why does she act like she thinks she owns you? And why do you believe every word she utters and leap to her defense all the time? Maybe my father better start watching the two of you very carefully."

With an explicit curse, Jared reached out and hauled her hard against him, his fingers digging into the delicate bones of her shoulders. "You better not have meant that to come out the way it sounded," he said, his voice deceptively low and caressing. "Because if you did, I'll. . . ."

"You'll what?" she challenged foolishly. "Toss me

into the pool and drown me before I tell Dad what I suspect?"

"You breathe one word of this nonsense to Jack and you'll wish I had drowned you," he threatened grimly. Dragging her up until her toes barely touched the tile, he growled down at her, "You can't really believe Delia and I are having an affair! You don't think I'd do that to Jack, do you?"

The hardening length of his body was issuing much more frightening warning than his mere words had conveyed and an inborn feminine instinct told her she dare not provoke him further. Impaled by his piercing gaze, she moved her head from side to side compulsively. "No," she confessed tremulously. "I don't really think you would do that to Dad. I . . . I did wonder about you and Delia when I first got here. I mean, she's always clinging so possessively to you that I thought . . . well, after I began to know you, I. . . ."

"Began to trust me a little? How gratifying," he taunted, his black eyes ablaze with impatience and something else that was undefinable. "And just what was it about me that changed your mind?"

"I don't know exactly," she retorted, resenting his mocking tone. "You just seemed too . . . honorable to do something despicable like that."

Somewhat appeased, he lowered her until her feet were flat on the tile again. His hands loosened their hold on her shoulders as he smiled down at her sardonically. "Little nitwit, how could you ever think Delia and I would be capable of betraying Jack?"

"Oh, I still think she's capable of betrayal," Suzanne replied tautly. "If you were willing, she'd be in your bed so fast, your head would spin."

"How can you be so sure of that?" he countered softly. "You don't really know what sort of person Delia is. She's nicer than you think."

Suzanne jerked away from him, balling her hands into fists at her sides. "There you go, defending her again! You're infuriating!"

"Temper, temper," he drawled. "You need to cool off." And in one fluid motion he scooped her up in his arms and tossed her into the pool.

Suzanne surfaced spluttering, the terry cloth robe dragging off her shoulders with the weight of the water it had absorbed. As she shrugged it off completely, Jared sliced through the water in a perfect dive from the side and she was waiting for him when he came up beside her. Balancing the soaked robe in one hand she plastered it against his face, laughing gleefully at the surprise she saw in his eyes before the robe hit him. "That's what you get for throwing me in," she taunted playfully, then gave a soft little gasp as he tossed the robe onto the edge of the pool and crooked a finger, beckoning her to him. "Come here," he commanded softly.

"I'm not crazy," she retorted and swam away as fast as she could.

It wasn't fast enough. Almost instantaneously, his hand closed around one slender ankle and she was being propelled backward in the silken water. When he dunked her, she clung to his arms, trying to pull him down with her but failing in that attempt, she was reduced to splashing water in his face when she surfaced. Their battle continued until she was too breathless with laughter to fight him any longer. While she clung by her fingertips to the pool's edge at the deep end and caught her breath, she watched him swim several laps back and forth. When he stopped, he still didn't seem tired and swam with long easy strokes to her. Her welcoming smile faded as he brushed against her, imprisoning her by holding on the edge around her with both hands so that she was in the circle of his arms.

She swallowed convulsively as his gaze traveled lazily down to the curve of her breasts, clearly outlined beneath the snug knit fabric of her swimsuit. Fire danced over her skin as if he had actually caressed her and she had never felt more vulnerable in her life.

"I'm tired," she said, her voice choked. "I think I'll take a little rest."

This time, he allowed her to swim a few yards, then suddenly caught her around her waist and dragged her back against him. Standing in water up to her shoulders now, she was grateful for something solid beneath her feet as he lowered his head and his breath caressed her ear. He was about to say something and anticipation mounted almost unbearably in her as she waited breathlessly.

"Suzanne," he finally murmured. "If I'd known you were such a good swimmer, I might have let you spend the night on the lake."

He was joking and she knew it. Sticking out the tip of her tongue at him, she splashed him, risking retaliation.

Retribution came swiftly but not in the same way as it had before. As his hands spanned her waist and he started to dunk her, she impulsively wrapped her arms around his neck. Her softly curved body bumped against his and, in that instant, playtime ended. A flaring passion replaced the amused glint in his black eyes as his long fingers spread open over her hips and pressed her against his hard thighs. "I *want* you," he muttered roughly. Then his mouth descended on her own with pillaging strength, parting her soft lips hungrily. In the silky water shimmering in the moonlight, she felt her body become all pliant femininity and she moved into his arms, yielding to his superior strength with fluid animal warmth. Her fingers curled into his wet thick hair as she kissed him back, her lips parting wider to the devouring pressure of his. Her mind whirled with the dizzying sensations he evoked. Her smooth shapely legs tangled with his and as the hardness of his lean body pressed against her thigh; she moaned softly.

Catching the full curve of her lower lip between his teeth, he played with her mouth, his warm breath filling her throat as he pushed the straps of her swimsuit from her shoulders. Gently insistent fingers slipped beneath the fabric. Then he was cupping the firmness of her breasts in his lean hands and she gasped softly as he caressed the tumescent peaks. She wanted him to never stop touching her. Moving feverishly against him, she stroked the taut tendons of his neck, whispering his name as he released her lips for an instant. He pulled back slightly and she gazed up at him with drowsy bewitching eyes. Trembling fingers grazed his face.

His jaw hardened beneath her fingertips and with a muffled exclamation, he put her away from him, stilling her hands as they tried to trail across his hair-roughened chest. "Go get dressed," he said hoarsely, raking his fingers through his hair. "Go, for heaven's sake!" Without gentleness, he pulled her straps back over her shoulders, then turned away.

She was so startled by his unexpectedly abrupt rejection that she got out of the pool automatically, hardly noticing that her legs were trembling as she walked back to the bathhouse. Once inside, she didn't even switch on the light and made her way to the end of the room in the dim illumination provided by the moon shining through the overhead skylight. Stripping off her swimsuit, she reached for a thick white towel. Shaking with reaction now, she clumsily tried to wrap it around her body sarong-fashion but before she could secure the end, the door opened.

Jared was a broad silhouetted form in the moonlit doorway. Her heart lurched and began to beat frantically but she took one step toward him. As she did, he stepped inside and pushed the door shut with his foot, closing them into the room together and closing out the rest of the world.

Still clutching the towel around her, she stood immobile as he came across the room. Her eyes widened to soft luminosity as she looked up at him and a shiver feathered along her spine though he made no move to touch her.

"Suzanne," he said huskily, slipping his hands beneath her jaw and cupping her face with exquisite tenderness. "You don't really know what it all means."

Her cheeks colored but she refused to look away and whispered, "I'm only inexperienced, Jared. I'm not ignorant."

With a groan, he swept her up in his arms and lowered her gently onto the wide sofa, coming down beside her, turning her to him. His lips sought her closing eyelids and the delicate hollows beneath her ears, his teeth tugging one tender lobe as he freed her hair from the elastic band. His fingers threaded through the braided strands, delighting in the silken texture. He trailed nibbling kisses along her cheek to her mouth, his lips warm, firm, plundering her softly curved shape with deepening intensity.

Touching tentatively, Suzanne's hands grazed across the muscular contours of his chest, then slipped down to stroke his lean sides—and Jared was not immune to such hesitant caresses. With a tortured exclamation, he rolled over, pressing her slender body down into the soft cushions, one long hard leg pinning both hers. The need to be closer to him flared within her and as she arched against him, one hand left her tousled hair to trail downward over her shoulders.

When his hand moved beneath the towel her breath

caught as his lean tan fingers traced the roseate peaks of her ivory breasts, teasing them to throbbing hardness. His lips followed the fiery trail his hand had blazed. She drew in a sharp breath and moaned with pleasure as his mouth closed on one taut nipple and pulled gently. As his hand spread open possessively across her satiny abdomen, an irresistible sense of inevitability overwhelmed her remaining inhibitions. Her arms encircled his waist.

"Oh, Jared," she breathed as his lips brushed hers again. "I love you."

He lifted his head, his eyes darkly unfathomable as he gazed down at her. "Suzanne," he groaned. "You—"

The bathhouse door suddenly crashed open, shattering the quiet and halting his words. The light flared on, blindingly bright. Instinctively clutching the towel up to her chin, Suzanne opened her eyes, blinking as she turned her head to stare bewilderedly across the room.

"So! This is the urgent business you had to attend to this evening, Jared?" Angelina exclaimed shrilly, anger flooding her face with crimson color. "Maria told me you were at the pool but I assumed you were alone. Hah!"

With admirable calm, Jared sat up on the edge of the sofa, saying nothing as he stared at the older woman. At last, his silent censure provoked a reaction. Angelina swore furiously at them in Italian, then swung around and slammed out of the bathhouse.

As a tremulous sigh escaped Suzanne, Jared looked down at her, his expression grim. "Tomorrow, you will thank her for accidentally rescuing you."

Totally unaware of how young and vulnerable she looked at that moment, Suzanne slowly shook her head. "Jared, I—"

'Get dressed,'' he interrupted flatly. "I'll take you home. It's too late to expect Maria to serve dinner. Do you mind?"

"No. I'm not hungry anyway but . . ."

"I'll be waiting outside for you," he muttered, then stood and strode across the room, pulling the door shut after him as he left.

Suzanne lowered her feet to the floor, shivering as her soles touched the cold marble. Dragging the towel, she went to the closet and began to dress. Her fingers shook as she raked them through her damp hair. She had never imagined she could love and need any man as much as she loved and needed Jared—and she hadn't even begun to dwell on the fact that he didn't love her. A few minutes ago, she had felt an incredibly intense joy in telling him she loved him. Then Angelina had appeared and reawakened nagging uncertainties. Yet, despite the uncertainty Suzanne felt, she doubted that she would ever want to thank Angelina for tonight's intrusion.

Chapter Nine

Stroking her sleek cap of black hair, Delia sniffed. "Well, frankly, I think you're taking advantage of Jared, Jack," she declared piously as her cold eyes cut around to sweep disapprovingly over her stepdaughter. "Suzanne can surely take care of herself one evening in Milan."

"But why should she have to spend the evening alone?" Jack Collins replied wearily, having gone through this argument before. "Since she has to meet Lynn's plane at 6:00 in the morning and he takes the flight to Rome at 6:10, they both have to spend the night in the city. So why shouldn't she ride down to Milan with him? I'm sure he doesn't mind at all. She'll be staying in the same hotel he is and he seemed willing enough to have dinner with her when I asked him to. He understands I'd rather she not spend the evening alone in a city she doesn't know."

"Well, did it ever occur to you he might have had other plans for tonight?" Delia asked irritably. "He has friends in Milan he probably wanted to see. I'm sure he isn't thrilled now that he'll have to baby-sit Suzanne."

"If he had made plans for this evening, I'm sure he would have said so," Jack retorted, his patience obviously wearing thin, "I didn't twist his arm. He certainly had the option of saying he couldn't."

At the foot of the stairs, Suzanne shifted the strap of

her straw purse from one shoulder to the other and moved her feet restlessly. She felt rather like a nonentity, being talked about as if she weren't even here. And she wished Delia would just shut up. From the moment she had heard Suzanne was riding with Jared to Milan this afternoon, she had vehemently voiced her disapproval of the plan. This seemed the hundredth time she had said Jared wouldn't want to waste his entire evening entertaining his partner's daughter and by now, Suzanne really felt as if she had been foisted on him. Uncertain as she was about his feelings for her, she didn't need Delia shooting off and making her feel even more insecure. It was distressing enough to realize Jared could never love her. She didn't want to incur his resentment by unwittingly interfering with his plans for tonight.

Trying not to hear Delia's repetitive words, Suzanne decided there was only one way to silence her stepmother. So, a minute later, when Jared returned to the gallery and announced that he had already put her suitcase in his car, she squared her shoulders and looked directly at him.

"Delia thinks having dinner with me this evening is probably upsetting other plans you made," she said abruptly, tugging at the lapels of her cream-colored jacket. "If that's true, please say so and I'll drive Dad's car to Milan. I don't want to cause you any inconvenience."

"Don't be ridiculous," was Jared's blunt answer as he placed his hands on his hips and practically glared at her. "Since we both have to go to Milan this afternoon, I think it would be more than a little foolish to take two cars, don't you?"

Frowning slightly, Jack stepped forward. "Delia has made me wonder if maybe I did put you on the spot when I asked you to spend this evening with Suzanne.

She's twenty-one—maybe I'm being too protective. If you have something else to do. . . ."

Jared waved him to silence. "You know me, Jack. If I'd had other plans for tonight, I certainly would have said so. Actually, I'll be delighted to have dinner with Suzanne."

So politely stated—rather like the required compliment given to the proud parents of an ugly baby Suzanne thought ruefully. Yet she did derive some satisfaction from the scowl on Delia's expertly made-up face. Obviously, she was displeased that her catty comments had ever been brought to Jared's attention.

"Are you ready to leave, Suzanne?" Jared prompted, glancing at his wristwatch. "If we go now, we'll miss the worst of the traffic."

Taking a deep breath, she smiled a good-bye to her father, then walked slowly across the gallery, barely controlling a tremor of excitement as Jared pressed his hand against the small of her back to allow her to precede him out the door. Since she hadn't really been alone with him in over a week—since that night in the bathhouse—she now felt shy, wondering if she had embarrassed him by saying she loved him. Perhaps he thought she hadn't meant what she said, that only the intensity of the moment had made her utter the words. Suzanne almost hoped he did think that. Though she still didn't regret what had nearly happened that night, she was somewhat sorry she had expressed her love for him in words. It was better to keep such feelings hidden, when there was no chance they could be returned.

As they stepped out from beneath the shaded portico into the bright late afternoon sunshine, she bent her head, veiling her eyes with the fringe of her lashes as if the glare of the sun bothered her. In actuality, she was trying to conceal the apprehension she felt about the coming hours. Jared seemed unusually tense and suddenly she was overwhelmed with the fear that he might be resenting her for ruining some plans he might have made for the evening. Finally she had to voice her uncertainty. As he opened the passenger door of the silver Jaguar sedan, she touched his arm tentatively and murmured, "Really, tell me the truth. Would you prefer not to have dinner with me tonight? If you don't want to, I . . . understand."

"Be quiet and get in the car," he snapped at her, practically forcing her down onto the black leather bucket seat. After slamming her door shut, he strode around to the driver's side and slid in beneath the steering wheel. After thrusting the key into the ignition switch, he paused before turning it. He looked over at her and seeing her chewing morosely on her lower lip, cursed beneath his breath. "You're acting as if you're the one who'd rather we didn't have dinner together tonight."

"I just don't want to inconvenience you."

"You aren't! Now, just forget anything Delia said and, for heaven's sake, try to relax," he growled, switching on the ignition. As the engine roared to life, one brown hand descended on the knob of the gear shift and he added in an uncharacteristically perturbed tone, "All right?"

Still gnawing on her lip, she could only nod, then turned to gaze blindly out her window for the next ten minutes until they had driven through Como and were speeding along the highway. She tried to make herself relax. Slipping her feet out of her shoes, she tucked her long slender legs up beside her on the seat as she turned sideways, closed her eyes, and nuzzled her left cheek against the leather. She had hoped to sleep but her nerves were too tautly strung to allow that. When five minutes or so had passed, she warily opened her eyes and gazed at Jared. His tanned face in profile was strongly carved and wholly masculine, though there was an enticing sensuality to the fuller curve of his lower lip. Trying not to remember how those lips could feel on hers, she closed her eyes again but compulsively reopened them almost immediately. He looked so tense, almost at odds with himself. He seemed constantly on the verge of saying something, yet he never said it. She had never seen him like this. Whenever she had irritated him in the past, he hadn't hesitated to come right out and say so. But now he seemed locked into a brooding silence that made dread drag at her stomach. If he was angry, she suspected that anger would erupt before the night ended and the longer he suppressed it, the worse the eruption would be.

Wisely, Jared had made their reservations at a deluxe hotel fairly near Linate airport and not too close to the hustle and bustle of Milan proper. At the entrance, while the parking attendant drove the Jaguar to the underground garage, Suzanne and Jared were ushered into the lobby by the doorman. This hotel was more modern than the one Jared had taken Suzanne and Delia to in Rome but Suzanne liked the decor here too, done all in earthtones of sand, ochre, brown and russet.

She had expected Jared to dump her straightaway in her room but he surprised her. After they registered at the desk, he requested that the clerk send their suitcases up to their rooms, then turned to catch her hand in his. "It's nearly six, not too early to have a drink. Come on."

She went willingly, hoping a drink would mellow him a little; to her relief he actually began to seem less tense even as they were walking into the bar. The English pub atmosphere was authenticated by the required dart board hanging on one wall. They took an oak table in a secluded corner and Jared removed his gray suit jacket and tossed it over the back of an empty chair before sitting down to Suzanne's right. The table was small. Their knees touched beneath it and Suzanne did not attempt to break that physical contact. Though she knew he felt very little for her, she still liked to be near him, especially now that he was no longer wearing a brooding expression.

The barmaid who came to serve them was distinctly Italian, despite the English pub atmosphere. She tossed her thick jet-black hair so that it swirled attractively against her olive cheeks and her warm brown eyes flirted outrageously with Jared. He didn't seem to mind and curiously, Suzanne discovered she didn't either. He was an attractive man. Young women would likely always flirt with him but she could stand to see him engage in friendly flirtations. It was his more serious involvements, like his relationship with Angelina, that tormented her. She shook her head, reassembling her thoughts. She didn't want to think about Angelina Sorveno right now.

After the barmaid had gone away again, Jared leaned back in his chair. "I hope you don't mind that I ordered a piña colada for you."

"Not at all. I had one once. I liked it."

"I've been told that they make very good ones here."

Nodding, Suzanne folded her hands demurely on the tabletop. "Perhaps I'll acquire a taste for them and won't always have to ask for white wine when I'm offered a drink. Maybe I'll seem more sophisticated."

"What a person drinks has very little to do with his or her degree of sophistication," Jared replied with a slight smile. "Besides, sophisticates often find the whole world boring and since you said you're never bored, you may never be able to describe yourself as sophisticated."

"I don't imagine you're bored very often either but you're not lacking in sophistication."

"I'm just a great deal older than you," he stated flatly.

"You're only twelve years older. I don't call that a great deal older."

"You think not?" he asked softly, his eyes narrowing. "I'm not so sure. You're such an innocent."

"I'm not as innocent now as I was before. . . ." She paused, not quite sure how to say exactly what she meant.

"Before what, Suzanne?" he prompted.

One of her small hands fluttered up then back down uncertainly. "Before I. . . ."

Jared laughed softly and touched his fingertips to her darkening cheeks. "You're proving my point: you are an innocent. You make it sound as if I were the first man who'd ever kissed you."

"Well, you're not," she muttered defensively, her rose-flushed cheeks seeming to belie her words. "I haven't been shut up in a closet, you know. I have been kissed."

"And?"

"And I never much cared for it," she answered bluntly, wanting to provoke some response other than amusement from him. "It's very different with you."

For the briefest instant, a light flared in the depths of his black eyes, then vanished as he grinned. "I'll take that as a compliment."

She almost winced. "I wish you wouldn't laugh at me. I don't appreciate being treated like a rather amusing child."

One lean brown hand covered both hers on the tabletop. "I think I'd better make a concerted effort to treat you that way tonight. Or—"

The barmaid arriving with their drinks interrupted

him and though Suzanne expected him to finish what he had been about to say when the girl went away again, he didn't. Instead he took a sip of his scotch and water and gazed at her intently over the rim of his glass. "Taste your drink, Suzanne," he then requested calmly, "and tell me what you think of it."

He had no intention of finishing the statement he had begun and knowing that, Suzanne suppressed a disappointed sigh and lifted the tall frosted glass before her. After a sip, she nodded. "It's very refreshing. I like the combination of coconut and pineapple."

After that they only talked about inconsequential matters, enabling Suzanne to relax. Jared was an interesting man, very knowledgeable in a variety of subjects and quite willing to hear and respect her thoughts. He had a delightful sense of humor and wasn't afraid to laugh at himself. His masculinity was naturally forceful but he never deliberately tried to project a tough macho image.

After an hour or so, when they had slowly finished their drinks, Jared reached for his coat. "I thought we'd have dinner early," he said. "There's a very nice roof garden restaurant here in the hotel—unless there's some other place you'd rather go."

Glancing back over her shoulder at him as they left the bar, she shook her head. "The roof garden restaurant sounds very nice. Besides, I wouldn't have any ideas about going somewhere else. I really know very little about Milan."

"You've never stopped over here long enough to see the sights?" he asked as they walked toward the bank of elevators in the lobby. When she shook her head again, he added, "We'll have to remedy that sometime. There are some magnificent cathedrals here I think you'd enjoy seeing. If you'd like, we'll drive down from Como some day soon and I'll show you around."

"I would like that," she replied, trying not to sound too eager. "If you're sure you have the time to bring me."

"Why are you always so anxious about time—especially mine?" he teased. "I'm beginning to think you believe I neglect my duties to the corporation."

"I know better than that. Dad's told me all about what you do—and in case you didn't know, he's very pleased with the partnership."

"I've never regretted our partnership either," Jared said sincerely. "Jack's a fine man. I have a lot of respect for him."

Suzanne felt he had put a barely discernible emphasis on those last words but when she looked up at him, she could see nothing unusual in his expression. After they stepped off the elevator on the sixth floor a moment later, Jared took both room keys from his pocket as they stopped in front of her door. "I've made the reservation for us at 8:30," he told her. "Will that give you enough time to get ready?"

She looked down at her mother's wristwatch, then shot a mischievous glance back up at him. "Good heavens, do I look so terrible that you think it'll take me a whole hour to make myself presentable?"

"I have no idea what your procedure is," he answered wryly. "Some women need half a day to get ready. Some don't."

"Well, I don't. In a pinch, I've been known to get out of the bathtub and out the door within ten minutes—fully dressed, of course."

Jared's dark brows lifted and amusement danced in his eyes. "You *are* a paragon of efficiency. Quite an attribute. So you'll be ready if I come by for you about 8:15?"

"Ready and waiting," she replied, watching as he unlocked her door for her. When he returned her key, his fingertips grazed her palm but she wisely showed no reaction and merely smiled as he started down the hall to his own room, three doors away.

Forty minutes later when he knocked, Suzanne, purse in hand, opened her door and switched off her room light simultaneously. Jared's face registered some surprise that she was actually completely ready but the mild surprise altered almost immediately to something else. His dark eyes swept over her, taking in the midnight blue tissue faille dress with its narrow braided straps, fitted bodice, and slightly gathered skirt that swirled attractively around her shapely legs. The color enhanced her creamy skin and the burnished copper of her hair, which she had swept back into a loose chignon on her nape, softening the effect by allowing a few wispy gold-lighted tendrils to graze her cheeks.

He said nothing, he didn't need to. The look in his eyes made her feel pretty—a relief, since he looked as disturbingly attractive as usual in a navy lightweight suit that accentuated his dark looks.

When the maître d' escorted them to their table five minutes later up in the rooftop garden, Suzanne noticed many feminine eyes following Jared then glancing at her with a hint of envy in their depths. They were given a secluded table for two near a narrow bed of white jasmine that bordered the perimeter of the roof. Lamps on posts at intervals provided soft illumination, assisted by single white candles enclosed in glass on each table. It was a moonless night but bejeweled by countless sparkling stars in the black velvet sky. Suzanne felt wonderful. She didn't know why—she just did. Every course of the meal was delicious, especially the magnificent prawns flown in fresh from the Adriatic, but after they had finished dinner and the music for dancing began, she fully expected Jared to suggest they leave.

Across the bright flame of the candle, his dark eyes sought and held hers. There was a certain hardening of his jawline that slowly relaxed as he looked at her. A half smile that seemed almost resigned fleetingly tugged at his lips, then he stood and held out his hand to her.

Without a moment's hesitation, Suzanne laid her fingers against his palm and felt almost as if she were floating instead of walking when he led her out onto the dance floor. Then his arms encircled her waist and hers lay on his broad shoulders and it was as if they had waited all day to hold each other. They had danced together before and it had been, for her at least, a sensual experience—but incomparable to this. Now that she knew Jared so much better and her feelings were so much stronger, being held so close in his arms was both torment and delight. He didn't speak. His hands didn't caress her except to occasionally stroke her hair. Yet she felt a need for him so intense that she was happy to go with him an hour later as he led her back to their table and handed her her purse.

He still said nothing as they took the elevator down to the sixth floor until, at her door when she handed him her key, her hand trembled. "Don't be afraid of me," he murmured, dark eyes holding hers. Then he turned the key in the lock and opened the door.

Her legs were curiously weak as she stepped into her room and as he followed and switched on the light, she turned back to face him, her green eyes widening. "C-couldn't we . . . I mean, the light . . . shouldn't we . . . leave it off?"

Shaking his head, he advanced toward her slowly, his gaze caressing as it swept over her. When she involuntarily took a backward step, he smiled gently, reached out and drew her into his arms. Taking her purse, he tossed it onto the bed behind them. He removed the pins from the chignon on her nape so that her hair tumbled down like a silken cascade over his hands and her shoulders. "I like it better down," he whispered. He gripped her slender waist lightly, squeezing and caressing, then reached around to lower the back zipper of her dress. Despite her soft startled intake of breath, he pushed the straps off her shoulders down her arms. The tissue faille rustled whisperingly as it drifted down to the floor around her feet. Now she stood in the circle of his arms in only a black half slip and a wisp of a black lace bra but when she began to tremble, he paused in the undressing.

Catching her chin between his thumb and forefinger, he tilted her face up and sought her mouth, teasing the sweet fullness of her lips with the firm touch of his until the aching need he evoked radiated throughout her body. "Oh, Jared, please," she breathed. "Really kiss me."

"You kiss me this time," he commanded, lean fingers tangling in her hair.

At first she was tentative, reaching up to touch the smooth skin of his neck but as desire overcame inhibitions, she caught his lean face between her hands, stretched up on tiptoe, and pressed her parted lips against his.

With a groan, he gathered her to him. His lips hardened, roughly capturing the soft shape of hers, the tip of his tongue tasting, then invading the opening sweetness of her mouth. The kisses they exchanged deepened, became a dangerous irresistible prelude to their passion. His mouth devoured hers. He held her so tightly against him that her feet no longer touched the floor and as she recognized the evidence of his desire, his virile strength conquered her, creating in her a pliant lassitude. Lowering her until her feet touched the floor again, he pulled off his tie, slipped out of his jacket, then pressed her hands to his shirtfront.

"Unbutton it," he huskily urged, watching as her shaking fingers opened his shirt and feathered across his bronze skin. His hands spanned her narrow waist, his thumbs stroking her bare midriff as he slowly drew her to the bed. Then he was beside her, looking down into her eyes. As if to reassure her, he touched his lips to hers gently, lazily arousing her ardent response. She pressed closer and with an urgent whispering of her name, he bore her down against the soft bed. Hardening lips took hers with marauding swiftness.

Turning over onto his side, he pulled her with him, his hands following the enticing arch of the small of her back. His fingers stroked upward along her spine, exploring the delicately boned structure of her back. Then the wispy lace bra came off and he took possession of her warm breasts, molding their softness against his palms, tracing the satiny nub-tipped peaks with his fingertips.

Fire danced over her skin and the hollow emptiness within became a nearly unbearable aching. Her hands beneath his shirt massaged his sides.

"Suzanne?" Jared whispered unevenly, asking everything of her as her eyes flickered open to meet his.

Her breath caught. A tremor shook her slight body but she gazed at him adoringly and touched a fingertip to each corner of his mouth.

He tensed. "I must be out of my mind," he groaned self-loathingly. "You're not ready for this, Suzanne. Your heart's about to leap out." The heel of his hand pressed down between her breasts. "I can feel it pounding."

She shook her head.

"Suzanne this is insane." he muttered, sitting up on the edge of the bed, brushing his thick dark hair back from his forehead. "Jack asked me to have dinner with you, not to spend the night in your bed. Some friend I am. I was afraid this might happen and I still allowed it to begin."

She touched his arm, dismayed when he stilled her hand and put it away from him. "But Jared, I. . . ."

He stood, looking down at her, his eyes narrowing when she instinctively covered her bare breasts with one arm and tugged down at the lace-edged hem of her slip that had twisted up to expose her slender, satin-textured thighs. With a muffled oath, he bent down to pull one side of the brown quilted bedspread over her, then straightened to rebutton his shirt. "How shy you are, Suzanne," he uttered roughly. "As I said, you're not ready for this."

There was a harshness in his tone that made her whisper bleakly, "I'm sorry you're so angry at me. I—"

"I'm not angry at *you!*" He wearily massaged the back of his neck with one hand. "Look, we have to talk about this."

"Yes," she said shakily. "All right. Then let's talk."

"Not now," he muttered, snatching up his coat from the foot of the bed. His narrowed gaze flicked over her once more and a muscle ticked in his clenched jaw. "No, definitely not now. It's late and we have to be up early in the morning. Good night, Suzanne."

Unable to utter a response, Suzanne watched him stride resolutely across the room and leave her. As the door closed behind him, she closed her eyes and pressed her fingers to her burning cheeks. He was right. This was insane. She loved him but he didn't love her and he seemed to understand better than she did how irrevocably hurt she would be if they had a brief affair.

The next morning at the airport, Lynn bounded through the gate and embraced Suzanne enthusiastically. "It's great to see you. I was beginning to think I'd never get here," she chattered. "Can you believe I stood in line at customs in Rome for over an hour. Thank goodness, I don't have to go through that here. There, they checked everything except my teeth. I don't know why. Maybe I look like some kind of disreputable character." As Suzanne laughed at her zaniness, Lynn glanced around, then feigned a look of outrageous surprise. "What's this? You mean the Empress didn't come to meet me! I'm shocked! I thought Delia was so crazy about me."

Though Suzanne couldn't help laughing she glanced over at Jared warily but he too was smiling at Lynn, despite her mildly sarcastic reference to Delia. Touching Lynn's shoulder, she turned her around and introduced her to Jared.

"A pleasure to meet you, Lynn," he said sincerely. "I hope you enjoy your visit to Como. I'm sorry to say I won't be seeing you for the first few days of your visit. I have to fly to Rome this morning." He glanced at his wristwatch. "In fact, I should be at the departure gate right now."

"Luckily, that's the next gate down from this one," Suzanne explained to Lynn as the three of them hurried along the wide corridor. They arrived at the boarding lounge with some time to spare and a tension came between Suzanne and Jared, a tension even Lynn sensed. An uncomfortable silence commenced until Jared reached for Suzanne's hand.

"Excuse us a moment, would you, Lynn?" he said calmly, then led Suzanne into the privacy of the nearest corner. Towering over her, he brushed a strand of russet hair back over her shoulder, his black eyes mysterious as they held her bemused gaze. "When I return from Rome Friday, I want to talk to you," he declared softly. "Okay?"

"Yes, okay, but Vito's sister's wedding is on Friday and we've been invited to spend the night at the Gallio villa in Bellagio so I'll be there. But I'm sure you've been invited too."

He nodded rather impatiently. "I do remember Angel mentioning it, yes, so I guess I'll go."

Did that mean he would be there *with* Angelina? Suzanne wondered bleakly, distress gathering in a painful knot in her chest. Bending her head to conceal the unhappiness she was certain showed in her eyes, she said softly, "So we can talk there, can't we? Could . . . would you tell me exactly what you want to talk about?"

"I think that's fairly obvious, don't you?" he responded grimly. "This situation is becoming intolerable and we have to straighten things out."

He was going to try to let her down easily. Suzanne was certain that was what he meant but she couldn't let him see how devastated she felt right now. Willing a little smile to curve her lips, she nodded. "All right, we'll talk."

"In three days then," he murmured. And when his flight was announced, he opened his mouth as if to say something, then changed his mind. His gaze was dark as he grazed a fingertip across her cheek, then lightly tapped the end of her small straight nose. Watching him stride away to the boarding gate, lithe and tall and dark in his tan vested suit, Suzanne drew a deep shuddering breath. If only she could fly back to Vermont before he returned from Rome. But she couldn't do that. She knew she couldn't She would simply have to brace herself for the moment when he told her finally that there could never be anything serious between them.

At last Suzanne remembered Lynn. Forcing a smile, she hurried over to her friend and began babbling. "We're taking the train to Como. I've never done that but I thought it would be a lot of fun. And on Friday, we're going to a lavish wedding at Bellagio, then spend the night in Vito's family's villa. I wrote to you about Vito. He's very eager to meet you. And I know you'll like him. Oh, we're really going to have a nice time while you're here."

Lynn eyed her speculatively. "Well, that all sounds terrific but I'll hear more about it later. Right now you have to tell me about Jared Caine. What's with you two?"

Suzanne heaved a sigh. "I'll tell you about it later, okay? I just can't talk about it now."

Lynn clicked her tongue against her cheek, her expression sympathetic. "It's that bad, hmm?"

"Worse," Suzanne confessed, then began chattering about Vito again.

Chapter Ten

Observing the excited sparkle in her friend's blue eyes, Suzanne smiled. "You really like Vito, don't you?"

Lynn sighed dreamily. "He's terrific. So dark and good looking and so . . . so wonderful. I really think I'm falling for him. And I think he likes me too, don't you?"

"Do you even have to ask me that?" Suzanne retorted with a grin. "Heavens, he's taken you out every evening since you got here and he calls you two or three times a day. I'm sure his work's suffering for it. What more can you ask?"

Lynn grimaced sheepishly. "Oh, I just feel insecure, I guess. After all I've only known him for three days." Upon hearing footsteps on the flagstone walkway in the garden where they sat, she nervously straightened the skirt of her dress. "Hush, here he comes now."

Smiling at both girls, Vito came to the bench where they were sitting, a certain special light appearing in his brown eyes as he looked down at Lynn. "Well, the bride and groom are off on their honeymoon and the reception is winding down so everyone can go home and have a little rest before the party tonight."

Lynn shook her head wonderingly. "I've been to some big weddings but this one sure takes the cake."

"'Takes the cake?'" Vito inquired, frowning bewilderedly.

"It means something is a prize winner," Lynn explained laughingly. "I meant that this is the grandest wedding celebration I've ever attended. There were hundreds of people at the ceremony and they all seemed to be invited to this spectacular reception. Then, to top it all off, there's a party tonight."

"My sister is the only daughter in our family and she is spoiled," Vito confided in a whisper. "My father wanted to give her the grandest wedding Bellagio has ever seen."

"Well, he succeeded," Suzanne spoke up. "I especially liked Sophia's dress. That was the most beautiful ivory silk I've ever seen."

"Woven in our own mill for my grandmother," Vito said proudly. "That was her wedding gown Sophia wore."

"Family traditions like that are nice," Lynn said, glancing back at the huge Gallio villa rising up behind them. "And it must be nice to live on the old family estate, especially one like this. The villa's magnificent, Vito."

He shrugged carelessly, assuming no self-aggrandizement because of his family's wealth and luxurious life-style. "It is a home," he said with more affection than pride. "I like to live here."

"I can see why. It's lovely," Lynn agreed. "Can you imagine how beautiful these gardens will look all alight tonight?"

"I hope you really do not mind that we will not stay long at the party," Vito said. "But this is the only time we can have dinner with my friend in Como. He and his wife will be leaving tomorrow for a long trip but insisted on meeting you before they go. I think you will like them."

"I'm sure I will," Lynn murmured, smiling happily as he took her hand and held it. "And I'd certainly rather meet close friends of yours than stay here at the party."

"But what about you, Suzanne?" Vito questioned. "Are you certain you want us to take you home on our way to Como? You will be there all alone. Why not stay here with Jack and Delia and enjoy the party?"

"No, I want to go home," she answered hastily. Though she had seen Jared at the wedding ceremony he hadn't talked to her yet as he had said he wanted to. But she knew that after hearing what he would say to her, she would be in no mood for a party tonight. So she had eagerly seized the opportunity to be taken home when Vito and Lynn drove back to Como. Now, as the couple talked softly together she gazed down at the azure waters below. At Bellagio, the three sections of the lake converged and all around, rolling green hills rose to splendid heights. It was a lovely place and she regretted feeling so downhearted during her first visit here. All her efforts to cheer herself had failed. She simply couldn't forget that Jared intended to tell her today that her feelings for him weren't and never could be reciprocated.

With a fairly convincing smile, she moved closer to the end of the bench to make room for Vito who sat down beside Lynn. Feeling they might want to be alone, she started to tell them she was going for a walk in the rose gardens but before she could stand, Angelina Sorveno came strolling along the pathway toward them. Suzanne groaned inwardly. Seeing Angelina was the last thing in the world she needed right now. The older girl had sat with Jared at the ceremony, clinging to his arm as if she meant to keep him by her side throughout the wedding festivities. Yet, now she was alone—through no fault of her own, Suzanne soon discovered.

"Has anyone seen Jared?" she asked haughtily, her

slow lazy gait causing her hips to sway provocatively beneath the skirt of her purple silk dress. After casting an unfriendly glance at Suzanne, she addressed her question to Vito. "Have you seen him anywhere? In the crush of people around the pavilion, we were separated and I do have something very amusing I wish to tell him." Chuckling suggestively, she cut her eyes in Suzanne's direction again as she continued, "I did not realize your moma is such an old-fashioned woman, Vito. She invited both Jared and me to stay over tonight after the party but . . ." she chuckled again, ". . . she actually gave us separate rooms. And I wouldn't upset her by telling her only one of those rooms will be occupied."

This deliberately hurtful revelation sickened Suzanne. To escape the triumphant glitter that appeared in Angelina's eyes, she turned her head to stare blindly at the yew hedge that bordered the rose garden, leaving Vito to deal with his sharp-tongued chief designer.

Fortunately for him, he didn't have to respond to her blatantly indiscreet comment because, at that moment, Jared came walking along the path toward the group. Suzanne tensed, wishing the earth would open up and swallow her as Angelina rushed to meet him, purring a welcome, and staked her claim by hooking her arms around one of his.

"I have been searching for you, *caro,*" she cooed. "I do not know how we became separated at the pavilion but now we are together so we can take that walk we discussed. *Si?*"

"Later, perhaps," he replied, ignoring her thoroughly displeased scowl. His narrowed gaze swept past Vito and Lynn to linger on Suzanne until she averted her eyes, as he added, "Why don't we all go back to the pavilion and have a drink to the bride and groom."

Though Vito and Lynn happily agreed to this idea,

Suzanne demurred. She had no desire to tag after the two couples, feeling like a fifth wheel. Besides, by avoiding Jared she could delay as long as possible the little discussion he wanted to have with her. Unable to look at him directly, she stood and gestured vaguely toward the flagstone path where it meandered through a small stand of lemon trees some distance away. "I saw Dad walking over there a moment ago so I think I'll go find him," she lied, managing to keep her voice steady. "I want to tell him something. The rest of you go ahead without me to the pavilion. I'll join you there in a few minutes."

"Oh, yes, let's do go on, *caro*," Angelina said with an exaggerated sigh. "The sun is so hot and I am so thirsty. A glass of champagne would be delectable right now."

Something akin to impatience registered on Jared's face but he nodded. "All right, we'll go without you, Suzanne, but we'll expect you to join us in a few minutes."

"Oh, yes, I'll be there," she lied again, then rushed away along the path as if in a great hurry to catch her father. The walkway curved around the far hedge surrounding the rose garden and, once out of sight of Jared and the others, she slowed her pace. For the next twenty minutes, she wandered through the gardens, stopping at last on a promontory overlooking the lake. A relatively secluded spot, it seemed the perfect place to wait until it was nearly six o'clock, the time when Vito planned to start back to Como. Although Suzanne didn't relish the prospect of spending over an hour alone with her dismal thoughts, she decided that was preferable to facing Jared and what he wanted to tell her.

Trailing her hand along the fragrant pittosporum

hedge, she walked to the end of the promontory. Low in the clear blue sky, the sun was casting a golden glow over the surface of the water and bronzing the villas set amid lush greenery on the far shore. The scenic beauty oddly intensified the aching constriction in her chest and she suddenly wished to be back in her drab little apartment in Vermont, where everything wouldn't remind her constantly of Jared. Yet such wishes were futile. She couldn't go home now and she knew it. Lynn had only been in Italy three days and since she and Vito were so obviously growing fonder of each other, Suzanne didn't want to spoil her friend's holiday. Surely she could bear to stay here a week or so longer, she told herself with a resolute uptilting of her chin.

Uncaring that she might stain the skirt of her ice-blue georgette dress, she sank down onto the cool grass near the edge of the promontory. A big black and white tour boat was leaving the quay in Bellagio, becoming smaller and smaller as it glided through the water, trailing a thinning wisp of gray from its smokestack. Watching it slip away, she plucked a blade of grass, idly twirling it between her fingers. She was so caught up in thought that she didn't realize she was no longer alone until Jared's deep voice sharply saying her name nearly caused her to leap out of her skin. She spun around, her eyes wide open and dilating with apprehension as she stared up at him towering above her.

"You said you'd join us at the pavilion," he said, his clipped tones denoting his displeasure. "You knew I wanted to talk to you today and yet you're hiding here, deliberately avoiding me."

The blade of grass slipped from her fingers as she gestured resignedly. "What's the point in talking? I already know what you're going to say."

"Do you really?" Swearing beneath his breath, he

sank down onto his knees beside her. "How on earth could you possibly know what I'm going to say when I don't know myself?"

Chewing her lower lip, she lifted her shoulders in a shrug. "Why bother saying anything? Why don't you just go back to Angelina? If you ignore her now, she might change her mind about the two of you sharing the same room . . . and bed tonight."

Hard hands gripped Suzanne's upper arms without gentleness and Jared glowered down at her. "You have a ridiculously overactive imagination. First, you decide I'm having an affair with Delia. Now, you have me sleeping with Angel. Where the devil do you get these adolescent notions? I'm not sharing a room with Angel tonight or any other night. I never have and I never intend to."

"Then why did she tell Vito, Lynn and me that you were?" Suzanne challenged heatedly, anger and hurt mingling to flash green fire in her eyes. "You don't have to lie to me, Jared. You're both adults and it's certainly none of my business what the two of you do together."

"Will you shut up and listen?" he ground out harshly, strong fingers biting down into her flesh to the small bones of her arm. "I don't care what Angel told you. She was lying. To me, she's a business associate and nothing else. How could you possibly believe I'd want to sleep with her when all I want is—" His words broke off abruptly and with a muffled exclamation, he shook his head. "I imagine she told that lie knowing you were naive enough to believe it—and she was right, wasn't she? And Delia's been right all the times she's not so subtly reminded me how young you are."

"I'm sick of hearing about Delia!" Suzanne exclaimed softly, twisting her body in an attempt to escape his iron hard grip. When he wouldn't release her, she went stiff and glared at him. "Don't you know she has a selfish motive for everything she does? She'd say anything to keep you all to herself!"

"I don't doubt that," he agreed astoundingly. "But she doesn't want to keep me to herself for the reason you think. You don't understand your stepmother, Suzanne. In her own way, she loves Jack and I don't think she'd ever be unfaithful to him. But she's weak and insecure and she needs the undivided attention of every man around her. Besides, she absolutely fell apart when Jack was ill so I took care of everything for her and she'd like to keep me to herself in the event she ever needs me that way again. But her selfish motive for reminding me how young you are doesn't mean what she says isn't true. You are too young, Suzanne, and that's what we have to discuss right now."

"Don't waste your breath," she murmured, bending her head, her gleaming titian hair falling forward to veil her cheeks. "I know what you're trying to do."

"I'm trying to be rational," he muttered savagely. "Heavens! Do you think I need Delia to tell me how young you are? I saw that for myself the moment you arrived here, vulnerable, lonely—unsure of even Jack's affection. I was the logical person for you to turn to, especially since I do such a lousy job of hiding how much . . . how attracted I am to you. It was probably inevitable that you would begin to attach too much importance to your feelings for me. This is a romantic place, especially for a young girl."

"My age has nothing to do with anything. I know you don't really think twenty-one is so very young."

"But it is, Suzanne. These days, most young women of twenty-one are still very unsettled."

"I'm not most twenty-one-year-olds," she uttered wearily, still staring down at the grass. "When Dad married Delia, I was sent to boarding school. I had friends there of course but there were no adults to really be close to so we all had to grow up fast. And I did, Jared. I'm not a frivolous person, looking for excitement anywhere I can find it. I know what I'm looking for. I want a sense of belonging . . . I want. . . . Oh, right now I just want to be back in Vermont."

"I think you'd be better off there too," he replied bluntly. "But since Jack wants you to stay here a few more weeks, I can only suggest we see as little of each other as possible." His hands on her gentled. "Suzanne, I think you need the next year to really examine your feelings for me. Then when you come back next summer, you'll be older. If you still think I'm the man you want, then we can take it from there."

She looked up at him, her eyes dark with reproach as she shook her head. "Don't play this game with me. Don't pretend you're giving me a chance to see if my feelings will change. They won't, though I know you wish they would. I'm sorry I embarrassed you by telling you how I felt that night in the bathhouse, but it's too late to change that now. I just wish you would stop trying to let me down easy. Just admit that you've only felt a physical attraction for me and that it can never be more serious than that. Just be honest with me, please. I can take . . . rejection."

"Rejection!" he exclaimed softly, cupping her face in his hands. "You idiot! Do you really think I *want* you to go back to Vermont? I don't want to give you this chance to change your mind, but I have to. I'm old enough and experienced enough to know what I want but you're not."

"You're just trying to be nice to me," she muttered bleakly. "You just don't want to come out and say I don't really interest you. But I'd rather you be honest."

"You want honesty?" he muttered unevenly, catching both her hands, drawing them to his white shirtfront beneath the lapels of his formal dark Oxford jacket.

His fingers pressed hers down against his hard chest as he said softly, "Feel my heartbeat. That's honest, Suzanne. Do you really think a desire to be nice to you could make it beat that fast? Don't you know what you do to me? You fascinate me. You're independent, yet sometimes you look as fragile as a flower. You're intelligent and amusing and the most desirable woman I've ever met. Now, how's that for honesty?"

Hope bloomed in her, a hope she felt compelled to suppress because she feared it was unfounded. Widening green eyes searched his lean face. "What are you saying, Jared?" she asked breathlessly at last. *"Exactly* what are you saying?"

"What am I saying!" he groaned, raising his eyes heavenward briefly, then gazing at her with such intensity that she trembled. And when she did, his self-control snapped. He pulled her roughly into his arms, his lips seeking the satiny skin of her throat. "Are you crazy? Don't you know yet? I love you, Suzanne, and if I could only believe your feelings for me would last. . . ."

"But I'll always love you, Jared! Please believe me," she implored softly, rising up onto her knees, sliding her arms around his waist to press closer to him. As he bent his dark head and his mouth took hers urgently, possessively, and the warmth of his strong virile body enveloped her, she surrendered eagerly. An exquisite joy made her dizzy with happiness. Jared loved her and somehow she was going to convince him her love for him was as real and lasting as his. Tangling her fingers in the thickness of his hair, she pulled away slightly to look up into his dark eyes. "It's you I want, Jared. There could never be anyone else. I know that."

"How can you know that, Suzanne?" he persisted, his narrowed gaze sweeping over her with possessive intensity. "If I can't convince you that you're too young, surely you have to admit you've never been seriously involved with a man before. So how do you know you're not just infatuated? Italy is conducive to romance and you were lonely when you arrived here. Maybe I was just available, convenient. Maybe you're overestimating what you feel for me."

"Oh, Jared, Vito was available and convenient too but I didn't fall in love with him." Tracing the hard contours of his face, Suzanne smiled tremulously. "Besides, he certainly gave me more encouragement than you ever have so if I was just lonely, why didn't I choose to love him? And I have been involved with a man before. Last year, I went out with a graduate student for several months. I liked him. I respected him. And sometimes, I even enjoyed his kisses but I never ever wanted him the way I want you because I didn't love him. He wanted to get serious and I didn't, so we stopped seeing each other. And I didn't ever even miss him. But, Jared, if you make me go back to Vermont and I can't see *you*, I think I'll die." She hesitated a moment, her cheeks coloring enchantingly. "I love you so much that I . . . well, you know, I wanted you to . . . oh, I don't know how to say it."

An indulgent smile tugged at the corners of his mouth. "I know what you mean. But if I'm the first man to awaken the passionate woman you are you might be mistaking physical attraction for love."

"There's an emotional need too, Jared, that's even stronger than the physical. I just need to be with you," she said simply, stroking his broad shoulders as she stretched up to press her lips against him. "Don't send me away. I don't need time. I just need you. Let me stay here where I can see you every day. Please."

"Suzanne, I love you," he muttered huskily, his long muscular arms closing tightly around her slender waist. Then his mouth descended on hers, exploring the soft shape of her lips, parting them with hardening demand as his hands caressed her throbbing breasts. As she wrapped her arms more tightly around him and gave him back kiss for kiss, he suddenly muttered her name roughly and held her away from him. "How can I possibly send you away when you respond to me like that?" he asked shakily, tracing the kiss-roughened outline of her lips with one fingertip. "But if you stay here, what about school?"

"Maybe I'll try for a career as a free-lance print designer," she answered happily. "Of course, I doubt Angelina will ever accept anything I do."

"I'm sure Vito could persuade her to judge your work with more objectivity. But would a career like that compensate for not going back to school?"

Just seeing you every day would compensate me, Jared. I do love you, whether you believe it or not."

Loving passion glimmered in his black eyes. "You're beginning to convince me. You're a very seductive woman without even trying to be—but now that you're being deliberately seductive, I don't think I can resist you much longer."

"Ah, ha, then I've accomplished my objective," she whispered, smiling mischievously. "You see, I'm enough of a woman to get what I want."

He drew her to him, cradling her in his arms, brushing a kiss against her shining hair. "All right, I can't fight you any longer. I need you too much to let you leave," he murmured softly. "And I love you too much to be satisfied with simply seeing you every day. So you'll just have to marry me. Okay?"

"When?" she asked eagerly, tilting her head back to gaze up at him, her green eyes softly luminous and adoring. "How soon?"

"An hour from now would be nice," he replied, smiling down at her. "But I'm sure we'll have to wait a little longer, unfortunately. I just hope it won't be too long. I'm not sure I'll be able to stay away from you many more nights."

"Who said you had to?" she whispered, touching slightly trembling fingers to his lean face.

Loving desire flared in his dark eyes but at last he shook his head. "That's a nearly irresistible invitation," he whispered back as his hands slipped beneath the petal sleeves of her dress, his fingers caressing satiny smooth skin. "But I'm certain Jack wouldn't approve— I'm not even sure he'll approve of our getting married."

"I think he will," Suzanne said, a tiny worried frown knitting her brow. "But what if he doesn't?"

"I'm afraid it wouldn't much matter," Jared confessed, smiling endearingly as he smoothed away her frown with gently stroking fingertips. "We are getting married, as soon as we possibly can. So Jack will simply have to realize you're no longer a little girl. You're a mature woman and since you've finally convinced me of that, I don't intend to wait to marry you. Falling in love has made me very possessive, Suzanne, and I need to begin sharing a life with you now."

"Sharing. What a wonderful word," she murmured, smiling softly up at him. And when he lowered his dark head to touch his lips to hers, she surrendered without hesitation, knowing at last exactly where she belonged —with him.

Silhouette *Romance*

THE NEW NAME IN LOVE STORIES

Six new titles every month bring you the best in romance. Set all over
the world, exciting and brand new stories about people falling in love:

27926 5	YESTERDAY'S SHADOW Sondra Stanford No.100	75p
27927 3	PLAYING WITH FIRE Laura Hardy No.101	75p
27928 1	WINNER TAKE ALL Brooke Hastings No.102	75p
27929 X	BY HONOUR BOUND Dorothy Cork No.103	75p
27930 3	WHERE THE HEART IS Donna Vitek No.104	75p
27931 1	MISTAKEN IDENTITY Laura Eden No.105	75p
27932 X	THE LANCASTER MEN Janet Dailey No.106	75p
27933 8	TEARS OF MORNING Laurey Bright No.107	75p
27934 6	FASCINATION Anne Hampson No.108	75p
27935 4	FIRE UNDER SNOW Dorothy Vernon No.109	75p
27936 2	A STRANGER'S WIFE Brenda Trent No.110	75p
27937 0	WAYWARD LOVER Barbara South No.111	75p
27938 9	WHISPER WIND Sondra Stanford No.112	75p
27939 7	WINTER BLOSSOM Dixie Browning No.113	75p
27940 0	PAINT ME RAINBOWS Fern Michaels No.114	75p
27941 9	A MAN FOR ALWAYS Nancy John No.115	75p
27942 7	AGAINST THE WIND Meredith Lindley No.116	75p
27943 5	MANHATTAN MASQUERADE Joanna Scott No.117	75p
28464 1	FOR THE LOVE OF GOD Janet Dailey No.118	75p
28465 X	DESIRE Anne Hampson No.119	75p
28466 8	TAKE THIS LOVE Mary Carroll No.120	75p
28467 6	JUST LIKE YESTERDAY Ruth Langan No.121	75p
28468 4	WINTERFIRE Carin Scofield No.122	75p
28469 2	HOLIDAY IN JAMAICA Tracy Sinclair No.123	75p

Silhouette *Romance*

THE NEW NAME IN LOVE STORIES

28633 4	SPOTLIGHT TO FAME Patti Beckman No.124	75p
28634 2	SWEET VENGEANCE Laurey Bright No.125	75p
28635 0	DREAM ONCE MORE Edith St. George No.126	75p
28636 9	BLITHE IMAGES Nora Roberts No.127	75p
28637 7	REALM OF THE PAGANS Anne Hampson No.128	75p
28638 5	MOONLIT PATH Jane Converse No.129	75p
32063 X	DREAM MASTER Laura Hardy No.130	75p
32064 8	TARNISHED VOWS Sondra Stanford No.131	75p
32065 6	BRIGHT TOMORROW Linda Wisdom No.132	75p
32066 4	SANDS OF XANADU Melanie Rowe No.133	75p
32067 2	MAGIC CRESCENDO Maggi Charles No.134	75p
32068 0	GAME OF HEARTS Sara Logan No.135	75p
32069 9	MAN WITHOUT HONOUR Anne Hampson No.136	75p
32070 2	ONE MORE TIME Elizabeth Hunter No.137	75p
32071 0	AMBER WINE Fran Wilson No.138	75p
32072 9	GARDEN OF THE MOONGATE Donna Vitek No.139	75p
32073 7	FORTUNES OF LOVE Helen Erskine No.140	75p
32074 5	CITY GIRL Arlene James No.141	75p
32687 5	RENEGADE PLAYER Dixie Browning No.142	85p
32688 3	SONG OF THE WEST Nora Roberts No.143	85p
32689 1	A NEW DAWN Ellen Goforth No.144	85p
32690 5	LOVE CAPTIVE Jacqueline Hope No.145	85p
32691 3	NIGHTSTAR Fern Michaels No.146	85p
32692 1	STARDUST Anne Hampson No.147	85p

Silhouette *Romance*

THE NEW NAME IN LOVE STORIES

32693 X	RELUCTANT DECEIVER Dorothy Cork No.148	85p
32694 8	THE KISSING TIME Jean Saunders No.149	85p
32695 6	A TOUCH OF FIRE Ann Major No.150	85p
32696 4	A KISS AND A PROMISE Anne Hampson No.151	85p
32697 2	UNDERCOVER GIRL Carole Halston No.152	85p
32698 0	WILDCATTER'S WOMAN Janet Dailey No. 153	85p
32722 7	DARING ENCOUNTER Patti Beckman No.154	85p
32723 5	DEVOTION Anne Hampson No.155	85p
32724 3	TIME REMEMBERED Lee Sawyer No.156	85p
32725 1	GAME OF CHANCE Donna Vitek No.157	85p
32726 X	AN OCEAN OF LOVE Elizabeth Reynolds No.158	85p
32727 8	YESTERDAY'S BRIDE Susan Tracy No.159	85p
32758 8	STRANGERS MAY MARRY Anne Hampson No. 160	85p
32759 6	RUN FROM HEARTACHE Brenda Trent No.161	85p
32760 X	ONE MAN FOR EVER Juliet Ashby No.162	85p
32761 8	SEARCH FOR LOVE Nora Roberts No.163	85p
32762 6	ISLAND ON THE HILL Dixie Browning No.164	85p
32763 4	ARRANGED MARRIAGE Brittany Young No.165	85p
32912 2	DREAMS FROM THE PAST Linda Wisdom No.166	85p
32913 0	A SILVER NUTMEG Elizabeth Hunter No.167	85p
32914 9	MOONLIGHT AND MEMORIES Eleni Carr No.168	85p
32915 7	LOVER COME BACK Joanna Scott No.169	85p
32916 5	A TREASURE OF LOVE Margaret Ripy No.170	85p
32917 3	LADY MOON Heather Hill No.171	85p

Silhouette Romance

EXCITING MEN,
EXCITING PLACES, HAPPY ENDINGS . . .

Contemporary romances for today's women

If there's room in your life for a little more romance,
SILHOUETTE ROMANCES are for you.

And you won't want to miss a single one so start
your collection now.

Each month, six very special love stories will be yours
from SILHOUETTE

33260 3	LOGIC OF THE HEART	Dixie Browning No.172	95p
33261 1	DEVIL'S BARGAIN	Elaine Camp No.173	95p
33262 X	FLIGHT TO ROMANCE	Tracy Sinclair No.174	95p
33263 8	IN NAME ONLY	Roxanne Jarrett No.175	95p
33265 4	THE SECOND TIME	Janet Dailey No.177	95p

All these books are available at your local bookshop or newsagent, or can be ordered direct from the publisher. Just tick the titles you want and fill in the form below.

Prices and availability subject to change without notice.

SILHOUETTE BOOKS, P.O. Box 11, Falmouth, Cornwall.

Please send cheque or postal order, and allow the following for postage and packing:

U.K. – 45p for one book, plus 20p for the second book, and 14p for each additional book ordered up to a £1.63 maximum.

B.F.P.O. and EIRE – 45p for the first book, plus 20p for the second book, and 14p per copy for the next 7 books, 8p per book thereafter.

OTHER OVERSEAS CUSTOMERS – 75p for the first book, plus 21p per copy for each additional book.

Name ....

Address ....

....